OCTOBER GOLD

Katie married Rhodri three weeks after they met. When they were stationed in Germany, and suffering a poison-pen campaign, she realised that she didn't know her husband. When Rhodri also heard of the campaign, his reaction was unexpected. Back in England, Katie became involved in a local murder. In a Kentish spring, Patrick came back into her life. But she had to return to Germany to discover the identity of the poison-pen writer and the direction of her own future.

MARY LANDY

OCTOBER GOLD

Complete and Unabridged

LINFORD
Leicester

First published in Great Britain in 1982 by
Robert Hale Limited
London

First Linford Edition
published 2006
by arrangement with
Robert Hale Limited
London

While some of the places in this book exist,
all the characters are imaginary.

British Library CIP Data

Landy, Mary
    October gold.—Large print ed.—
    Linford romance library
    1. Love stories
    2. Large type books
    I. Title
    823.9'14 [F]

    ISBN 1–84617–410–4

Published by
F. A. Thorpe (Publishing)
Anstey, Leicestershire

Set by Words & Graphics Ltd.
Anstey, Leicestershire
Printed and bound in Great Britain by
T. J. International Ltd., Padstow, Cornwall

This book is printed on acid-free paper

For

Jimmy and Valerie Knight

Part One

1

Katie was the first to realise that something was wrong. Till then the party had been just like any other, moderately successful and entirely predictable. The hostess had probably spent most of the afternoon making the canapés and persuading herself that they were noticeably different from anyone else's. The drinks were strong. Most of the wives had tarted up last season's cocktail dresses with jewelled belts or collars. The only new one belonged to the hostess. After all, it was her party. Katie's glance roved round the room looking for the not quite suitable striped chiffon and suddenly knew that she hadn't seen it for some time. Claire had disappeared.

★ ★ ★

There weren't many places where Claire could be if she was still in the house. Katie abandoned her half-hearted exchanges with a man she met only — and too often — at parties like these, and squeezed her way out of the room. She glanced automatically into the kitchen where Barney, Claire's sixteen-year-old son, was demolishing a plateful of tiny sausages, and checked that there was no one in the downstairs cloakroom. There was nowhere else but the cellar, which was unlikely, or upstairs. Katie thought of calling up and decided against it. She put a tentative foot on the first step. Then she saw the envelope on the hall table. It had been thrown down, opened side uppermost, as if someone had pulled out a note and gone away to read it in private. Upstairs? There was nothing about the envelope to indicate that the letter was anything special but, even before she picked it up, Katie knew that she was going to recognise the hand-writing. Not that she could relate it to a specific person, just that she had seen it before. The last time it had been addressed to herself, and the signature at the bottom of the single sheet of writing paper had been NEMESIS.

Barney had progressed to the savoury dip, using a tablespoon instead of the more conventional biscuits or crisps. One of Claire's touches, Katie had noticed, were florets of cauliflower, equally ignored by Barney.

'How long have you been here?' Katie asked.

'Since forever. I'm supposed to open the front door.'

'You wouldn't remember when this was left on the hall table, would you?' Katie dangled the envelope in front of him. He glanced at it incuriously. 'Someone must have dropped it there while I was hanging up coats.'

'Any idea who it was?' Katie asked casually. It was too much to hope, she knew. Whoever was responsible for the present outbreak of anonymous letters was unlikely to leave anything to chance.

'No.' Barney's eyes strayed in the direction of a large tray covered with silver foil.

'Someone did bring it, though? It didn't come through the letter-box?' Katie could feel her fingernails digging into the palms of her hands. It was terribly important to find out now if Barney could tell her anything because this was the only opportunity she was going to have. Apart from the fact that half-term was nearly over, it wasn't the sort of topic one could ever broach again.

'No — I'd have heard that. Tell you something, though. It wasn't there when Colonel Darran left the bottle of wine on the hall table.'

★ ★ ★

There obviously wasn't going to be anything else to be got from that source. Katie, still worried about Claire, tucked her long black hair back behind her ears and advanced purposefully to the foot of the staircase. At that moment Mark Fordyn swept out of the sitting-room and into the kitchen. 'What the hell's happened to the food?' Katie couldn't see him from where she stood but she could imagine those well-bred features tightened with irritation, the dark eyes narrowed. 'And where's your mother?' he snapped.

'She went upstairs,' said Barney with monumental indifference.

'Then get off your bottom and start handing things round . . . ' One of the now commonplace family rows started to run its familiar course. Katie waited in the shadows of the hall, ready to disappear if Mark should go in search of his wife. Only a yard or so from the table, her eyes wandered over its contents. Telephone, ashtray, clothes brush, a small parcel wrapped in coloured paper, a bottle of wine. It was a Rhein wine in a tall, slim bottle . . . Mark stalked back into the living-room, followed by Barney carrying the large tray. Katie waited for a moment, listening for a sound from the rooms above. Then she started slowly up the stairs, her black taffeta skirt whispering round her legs. Below her, voices rose and fell in a steady hum, a man coughed, someone laughed rather too loudly. Mark could be heard calling to Barney. Kate reached the landing. The guest-room being used for parking coats was straight ahead. The next one, smaller, could only belong to a teenager. Between that and the bathroom were the doors of the main bedroom and its adjoining dressing-room. Both were shut. The only light came filtering through from what was obviously a bedside lamp in the guestroom. Caught by indecision, Katie moved in there and looked at her troubled face in the mirror. Had she any right to interfere? Wouldn't it be better to leave things as they were?

★   ★   ★

Claire put the letter down, dry-eyed. After all, it only spelt out what she already knew. In fact, the statement it contained wasn't even true. 'Wives are always the last to know, aren't they?' It was signed in block capitals, as was written the address on the envelope. The message was made up of pieces of newsprint glued together. The whole thing, she thought dispassionately, had an amateurish look. But there was nothing unprofessional about the whole campaign. She moved over to the dressing-table and pushed the sheet of paper to the back of her make-up drawer. Her eyes looked sombrely back at her. Brown hair, auburn-tinged when newly washed, was parted in the middle, emphasised the oval of her face. Not quite as slim as she used to be but still a pretty woman. Mark had once found her beautiful . . . She wrenched her thoughts away from that. She decided she had been up here long enough. Briefly she wondered if Mark had missed her and came to the inescapable conclusion that, if he had, it was only because nobody had come bounding in with the hot sausages. She choked down the usual feeling of sick misery, and opened the bedroom door.

Katie heard it open and stayed where she was. There was little she could say to comfort Claire. It might have helped a bit for her to find she wasn't the only sufferer but Katie weighed that against the disadvantage of anyone, however friendly, knowing about the letters she herself had received and came down firmly on the side of discretion. She waited another couple of minutes and then went back to the party. The noise by now had crept up a decibel or two. Mark's heavy hand with the gin and whisky was having its effect. Several faces were flushed, eyes unnaturally bright, voices becoming shrill as they fought to be heard. There were too many people per square foot and there was too much cigarette smoke for the height of the ceiling. After the next few minutes, Katie found, a merciful deafness intervened. She gave up testing her larynx and looked around for Patrick Darran. It didn't take her more than twenty seconds to discover he had gone.

Claire was talking to two comparative strangers when Katie went over to join her. People were beginning to drift away, saying goodbye, calling to husbands or wives, taking their coats from a suspiciously helpful Barney. The cold, frosty air of late October streamed in through the open door. 'I've hardly seen you at all,' Claire said brightly. 'Must you go? Oh — did you know? That bottle of wine on the hall table is for you. At least, it's got your name on it.' Katie said the obligatory what-a-lovely-party, picked up her coat, collected the long, slender bottle and walked the hundred-odd yards up the road to the house she called home.

In the warm, square kitchen which overlooked the playing fields and the Church of St. Benedikt, she scrambled eggs and tracked down the corkscrew.

As she ate, she sipped a glass of wine and thought about Patrick. This considerate gesture was a far cry from the days they had played and fought and gone to school together in a village just over the hill from Killarney. A lot of water had flowed under Rossmara bridge since then . . .

★ ★ ★

Down the road, at the house on the corner, the front door closed on the last departing guest. Claire knew that she had kept him too long, chatting desperately in the hall, afraid of shutting out the world. Barney was already barricaded into his room. That left Mark and herself. Silently they started to clear away the debris, stacking plates and glasses, emptying ashtrays. She thought of the last party they'd given and tears stung her eyes. Then they had, as always before, closed the door thankfully and sunk into armchairs for a final drink and a thoroughly enjoyable analysis of the clothes, manners and alcoholic intake of their recent guests.

'You're not doing this stuff tonight, are you?' Mark asked perfunctorily, heading out of the kitchen. 'Think I'll run up to the club for an hour. Alright?' It didn't matter, Claire thought bitterly, if she answered or not. He would go anyway — and almost certainly not to the club. Oh, he'd probably look in there, just to be seen, and then drive round to where Joanna lived . . . She turned towards the window, fiercely pressing her lips together. Whatever happened she had determined to avoid a scene. There were things which, put into words, could never be retracted. If she just went on being pleasant and good-humoured, the whole horrible thing would go away, and she and Mark could return to the old affectionate, easy-going way of life. Sometimes she wished she was brave enough to put to the test all that they'd built up over the years, but she knew she'd never do it as long as there was a chance that this affair was merely the reaction of a man who suddenly realises he is approaching middle age. *Torschlusspanik*, the Germans called it — the panic of closing doors. His career was predictable, his relationships settled: his son was now the person who had the power to choose.

Reminded of Barney, Claire went slowly upstairs and opened the door of his room. The mess was indescribable. Exercise books, posters, cut-outs from magazines, paste, glue, scotch tape, two model aeroplanes, a pair of football boots, a dressing-gown cord, chewing-gum wrappers — on the bed, on the chest, on the only chair. In the midst of it all, Barney sat on the floor, plucking at his guitar. A thatch of fair hair fell over his forehead: he had changed back into his favourite gear, frayed jeans and a shapeless T-shirt. 'Anything left to eat?' he asked hopefully.

Mark Fordyn knew exactly what

evenings he could expect to find Joanna on her own. He left his car in a parallel street, then walked down the cul-de-sac to the last semi-detached house on the left. Beyond lay the path through the woods where he had first seen her. Even then, on a gloomy day in March reaching towards dusk, he had noticed the face as something different in a typecast society. When he met her again, as wife of a subordinate, he recognised her immediately. Since then that candid face, the half-parted lips and the little-girl mannerisms had never ceased to enchant him. To invite her and Colin to the house was the natural thing to do: for them to reciprocate was in the normal course of events. Subsequently, Mark had no trouble in finding plausible reasons for calling at the house when Colin was elsewhere. The first time he held Joanna in his arms, he felt as if the hands of time had been reversed and he wasn't much older than Barney, with all his dreams still in front of him.

She opened the door to his ring, her silky hair an aureole against the light inside. In the hall, she clung to him.

'Oh, Mark,' she whimpered, 'I've had such a horrid letter.'

2

It wasn't till next morning that Katie realised the opportunity she had missed. Her first thought on waking in the wide double bed was that Rhodri would be back the day after tomorrow. The second — that there wasn't much time left. She had known last night that the poison-pen writer was actually there at the party. That in itself didn't make things much easier because there had been at least fifty people milling around from sitting-room to dining-room. But she had even been given a clue. The letter addressed to Claire had not been on the hall table when Colonel Darran deposited the bottle of wine. Too late, she had tried to find out if he had any idea of the time he arrived. She could telephone him, of course, but surely he'd want to know the reason for such an unexpected question? Even if he didn't ask for an explanation, he would remember the request. No — better to ask, in a casual way, host and hostess whom he would naturally have sought out first. But better make it soon . . .

★   ★   ★

Those were the words she had used, silently, when someone turned his head in a crowded bar and looked straight at her. It had been instant attraction. The setting was Twickenham, nearly three years ago, England versus Wales. She and a gang from the university were having a quick drink before the start. He, in a circle of lilting voices, could only be Welsh. At any moment the crowd would shift and they would never see each other again . . . When a deep-chested roar signalled the emergence of the teams, the spectators surged towards the stands. She saw a square, humorous face under straight dark brown hair — a face, oddly, that seemed as familiar as if she'd known it a long time. She heard his voice just before she was swept away. 'Rhodri Rees-Williams,' he shouted. Not an easy name to forget. She couldn't know it was the name she was going to marry.

She hadn't expected him to be in the London telephone directory but he was.

'What would you have done if I hadn't been listed?' he asked her when he called to take her out to lunch next day. Katie had given it some thought.

'London Welsh,' she replied promptly. 'You'd have left a message there for me there, wouldn't you?'

'The first thing I did after the match.' He looked at the shining sweep of black hair and the wide-set smoky blue eyes. 'I've been wed before,' he said, 'and I swear I'm ten years older than you. We'd better drink champagne, don't you think?'

They got married three weeks later and went to live at his house in — appropriately — Twickenham. 'Not Twickers itself,' said Rhodri, 'just the postal district.' He had a tall, narrow, three-storied house near the river. From the first floor living-room, you could see the water; from the main bedroom, the willows which fringed the Surrey shore. The house in between his and the bank had a garden which blazed with colour from April till October. 'All the pleasure,' said Rhodri, 'and none of the work.' Harlech House ('truly I didn't re-name it,' protested Rhodri) was crammed with books from ground-floor kitchen to attic bedroom.

'What I'm sure you don't want, and what you're going to have,' said Katie, 'is a woman's touch.' She cleared out the living-room, painted the walls magnolia white. Then she covered the chairs in grey-blue linen and hung her Paul Henry originals on the walls. The misty blue hills and grey-edged clouds of Donegal and Connemara reflected the shimmer of the Thames below, the daffodil-yellow curtains absorbed the sunlight. 'Not even a Welshman could have done it better,' admitted Rhodri.

When he was posted to Germany, Katie gave up her research job at London University and they let the house.

'We can't leave it empty,' said Rhodri. 'Squatters, vandals, misunderstood teenagers . . . '

'With a permissive society,' agreed Katie, 'who needs enemies?'

So they found a colleague of Rhodri's willing to take it on for a provisional two years. There was no doubt in their minds that they'd eventually be returning to Harlech House together.

★ ★ ★

After a year and a half in Germany, Katie reckoned there wasn't much she didn't know about an Army camp. There were few suicides at Niederdorf but there was a steady flow at the psychiatric clinic. The discontent of wives with too little to do; the restrictions of a cantonment, the language barrier outside; young typists

and teachers expecting continental
gaiety and finding the drab monotony
of a hostel lounge; the lure of duty-free
spirits and inexpensive wine. So many
reasons for disenchantment. Yet everything was provided. Apart from a
NAAFI which sold steam yachts as well
as instant coffee, there was a block of
German shops, there were churches,
playing fields, an Olympic-size swim-
ming pool, two cinemas, bars for
officers, sergeants and corporals. There
were classes in pottery, dressmaking,
car maintenance and housewives'
German. There were clubs — social,
educational, sporting. There were teen-
age discos, bingo nights, curry lunches,
endless farewell parties. Some people
suffered from mental claustrophobia.
The majority wouldn't know what it
meant.

After coffee and toast and a mini-
mum of housework, Katie shopped at
the NAAFI and then went along to call
on Claire. The side door was open so
she knocked perfunctorily and walked

in. The kitchen seemed to be full of glasses, some washed and dried and stacked on trays, some on the draining-board, others in the sink. One was smashed on the Marley tiles. Claire slumped in a chair, her head on the table. She was crying. So lost was she in a private grief that she wasn't even aware she was no longer alone. Katie hesitated. Claire was quite a bit older, she wasn't a close friend, they hadn't really got a lot in common. Also, she was a reticent person, the kind who believed in keeping her troubles to herself. She would not easily forgive an intrusion. Katie, her soft suede boots making no sound, slipped out again. She couldn't just abandon Claire, especially with what looked like all the party debris plus the breakfast dishes to cope with. But she could give her time to recover. She would walk across the playing fields and back.

The forest from which the camp had been carved was never far away, and the trees to the south-west stretched in an unbroken line. A burst of sun hit the leaves in a swathe of saffron and bronze, brilliant against the stormcloud beyond. It was a wild, adventurous sort of day. There was a longing for escape, escape with Rhodri from the flat and featureless Rhineland, away into Holland, past the windmills and the dykes and on to the coast; there to stand on the windswept dunes and walk by the tumbled waves of the grey North Sea . . . But Rhodri wasn't here. Even if he were, he wouldn't want to come with her. Not if he knew what she'd done.

She went back to the kitchen door and lifted her hand to knock once more. But this time Claire obviously wasn't alone. Someone else was speaking, then Claire's voice answering. Too late to retreat. She opened the door and stepped into the kitchen. 'Claire, I came to see if I could help. Oh, hullo, Margaret!' Margaret Tolworthy smiled briefly and continued to polish glasses. Katie, as so often before, was aware of the invisible barrier which existed between Army and civilian wives in a predominantly Service environment. 'They regard us as second-class citizens,' she'd once said to Rhodri. He had laughed. Rhodri's job was Intelligence and he didn't wear uniform. 'That's because we don't give a damn,' he'd said, 'and they have to keep jockeying for position.' At least Margaret's position, thought Katie, was practically unassailable. Brigadier Tolworthy had no further to go; his next post was honourable retirement.

'You've done it nearly all,' said Katie. 'Can't I help at all?'

'Any competent housewife would have done it last night,' answered Claire. She was wearing dark glasses but otherwise appeared brisk and pleasant as usual.

'Anyway, do stay for coffee,' she went on. 'I'd invited Margaret and meant to get this all out of the way first'. She plugged in the percolator and set a tray neatly with three cups and saucers, cream and brown sugar and a plate of biscuits. She does it all automatically, Katie reflected, the real coffee, the homemade biscuits, the rose-patterned china. She followed two impeccably-clad tweed-skirted posteriors into the sitting-room. She wondered if they ever slopped around, as she did, in jeans and their husbands' old shirts. Certainly not Margaret. She hadn't the figure. But maybe Claire was unconsciously influenced by her son when nobody else was around.

'Has Barney got a girl-friend?' she asked. Claire, pouring out with her left hand and offering cream and sugar with the other, managed a shrug of the shoulders. 'Only one at the moment, Lindy Grey. I think she's rather a bright child, nearly seventeen, needing more scope for her talents than the average Army school. Her father's a teacher, divorced I think, and likes to keep her under his eye. Barney,' she added drily, 'has other ideas.'

'Does she come into his future?' Katie asked.

'Not unless her ambition is an overland journey to India, returning by way of the Himalayas.'

'There's something to be said for a son at Sandhurst,' commented Margaret Tolworthy. 'Not so much time for leisure activities.'

'And a daughter in Canada, haven't you?' Claire passed round the biscuits. Margaret asked for the recipe. Katie wondered how she could switch normal coffee-party conversation round to what she wanted to know. Finally she remarked how good the party food had been 'Incidentally, I wanted to have a word with Patrick Darran,' she added, 'but he'd gone. Do you remember when he arrived, Claire? I never saw him at all.'

'I think he must have been one of the last,' Claire said doubtfully. 'Yes, I remember now. He could only stay a short time because he'd booked a long-distance call from the Mess. I think he came in just in front of you, didn't he, Margaret? By the way, are we playing together tomorrow?' The talk drifted on to golf. Katie finished her coffee and stood up to go. 'No, I won't be driving out with you and Margaret tomorrow,' she said to Claire at the door.

'I have to go to the dentist.' It had to be something dire to convince the other members that absence was unavoidable on Ladies' Day at Tolrath Golf Club. Claire and Margaret accepted the lie, though obviously contemptuous of the folly of fixing an appointment for a Thursday morning. A year ago, Katie might have said that she had better things to do. But she had learnt since then that a measure of conformity was essential in a closed community. Also, she wasn't sure if what she had in mind was strictly legal.

★ ★ ★

Tampering with Her Majesty's mails, it would be called in England. Katie didn't doubt that there was a word for

28

it in German and that it wouldn't be a short one. Not that there was any chance that she could interfere with the workings of the German post office but, by way of a little ingenuity and a small cash outlay, she might be able to find out who was using it for the transport of poison-pen letters.

The two she had received were in her handbag. And wherever she went, her handbag accompanied her. Whatever happened, Rhodri must never read them. Whatever ensued, there must never come a time when another envelope carefully addressed in block capitals should fall through the letter-box when Rhodri was there to pick it up. So far she had had nothing to work on. Now at last she had a workable plan. Both her letters had been delivered by the German postman on a Friday morning between ten and ten-thirty a.m. That meant they had been posted on Thursday afternoon. She now had a mental list of all last night's guests. Most of them could be eliminated; about seven were possibilities. If one of the possibles were to insert a letter into the yellow box outside the *Postamt* on Thursday any time after noon, there was an outside chance it was the person she was seeking.

She couldn't know then — and would never have guessed — the surprising result of the first vigil.

3

The remaining hours of Wednesday stretched ahead. Restless, Katie wandered round the house, knowing only that some sort of action was imperative. Suppose she'd been wrong in her assumption that Thursday afternoon was the operative time? What then? The obvious line was some sort of general surveillance of the German post office, but as that was open from eight-thirty to five-thirty daily, nothing short of camping in the B.P. garage opposite could yield results. That was where Gary came into it. Gary was the son of one of her more matronly golfing friends, currently doing a stint there to earn some pre-university pocket money. A few extra Deutschmarks a day would probably come in very useful.

Rhodri had gone to Berlin by air, so the car was in the garage. Katie backed it out and drove along to the B.P. petrol pumps. Fortunately Gary was on duty and fortunately Gary was looking bored. It was the slack time of the morning.

'Fill her up, will you, Gary?' She sat, watching his languid movements. 'And if you've a spare moment now and again, could you do something for me? For a fee, of course,' she added hastily. He looked fractionally more alert. 'You see the *Postamt*?' He could hardly fail there — it wasn't more than twenty yards away. 'Could you — when you aren't too busy, of course — make a note of any woman you know putting a letter into the box for, say, the next week?'

That wasn't as forlorn a hope as it sounded. Gary's family had been on the camp for nearly three years and they knew a lot of people. More important, his mother used to tote him round as a caddy — as Claire sometimes did with a reluctant Barney — so he knew most of the Golf Club members. Six out of the seven possibles on the list belonged to the Club, five of them women. Instinctively Katie knew that the writer had to be a woman.

She felt that some explanation was due to her new employee. 'I'm writing a detective story and I want to test out a theory. Nobody knows about it, even my husband, so absolute secrecy is a condition of the — er — retainer.' The last word seemed to ring a bell. 'Five marks a day,' said Gary. She looked at him with respect. Five marks was getting on for a hundred and twenty pence. She could see a great future for the lad. 'Three,' she said firmly. He took the coupons for the petrol and slouched back into the shelter behind the pumps. She got into the car. 'Gary!' she called. He came over, wallet at the ready. 'Here's the first instalment. Incidentally, I'll take over tomorrow afternoon, just to get the feel of it. Don't take any notice of me.'

Looking back later she realised that she still, at that stage, had hope of

clearing the whole thing up within a
few days. Such confidence was the only
alternative to a bleak and unknown
future.

★　★　★

The first letter she'd received could
have been beginner's luck on the part
of the writer, a shot in the dark. Most
people had something to hide, and
many would read their own guilt into
an anonymous threat. 'Who were you
meeting that night in the woods?'
asked a pasted-together conglomera-
tion of words. The envelope, addressed
to Mrs K. Rees-Williams, 603 Niederdorf, 13 Acacia Avenue, was written in
block capitals. It was a question which
one could, even if slightly uneasy,
ignore. The second one was more
specific. 'Shadowers can be shadowed,
you know.' It also had been signed
NEMESIS. That one, Katie had reason
to suspect, spoke of definite knowledge. She remembered that evening

only too well. The woods at the rear of the camp deepened into what had once been a sizeable forest. She had walked further than usual, right off the beaten track. The wind was still sighing in the tops of the pine trees but there was an eerie stillness below. Her feet made no sound on the soft carpet of needles. The premature dusk made her suddenly afraid — that and the feeling that she had closed up too abruptly ... Oh yes, it was true alright. Somebody must have been following her. But who could possibly have known her intention?

★   ★   ★

It was a windy day, with great fleecy clouds bowling over a limitless expanse of sky. Katie made a sandwich, drank a cup of coffee and decided to go out to the Golf Club. There would certainly be more men there than women, as Wednesday afternoon was usually devoted to sport in the Army, but she might find someone to play with and/or pick up a clue. As she drove fast down a straight, level German road she reflected that few occasions were more conducive to confidences than a three-hour slog round a golf course. Even if one's partner wasn't a friend — in fact, especially if she were a comparative stranger — one was apt to say things which, pieced together, could be of great use to a potential blackmailer.

The Ladies' Locker Room was cold and empty. It only came to life on Thursday mornings when between nine and nine-thirty they all trooped in — blonde and dark and subtle shades of grey; the confident, the beginners, the also-ran who declared they only played for the exercise. Names like Katie, Claire, Margaret, Susan, Sarah, Veronica, with husbands on various rungs of the Army ladder or in the many affiliated civilian organisations. Thursday morning was the only time in the week when rank gave way to individual performance and where, under the handicapping system, everyone had a chance to shine. It was a freemasonry unlike any other on the camp, and it looked as if someone was abusing that easy camaraderie.

It was Veronica who turned up just as Katie was ambling towards the first tee. Her husband was the gynaecologist at the local Army hospital. All the lady members knew, from Veronica's moanings, how she regretted her failure to engage his professional interest. Katie foresaw an obstetrical afternoon.

By the ninth, Katie was two up. Veronica was a brilliant, if erratic, player and today she obviously had something on her mind. The usual, one suspected. She strode round the course, broad hips ('so suitable for child-bearing, my dear') swinging, eyebrows drawn together under a thick auburn fringe. She hardly spoke at all. Her breaking point came at the short eleventh. More than one person's breaking-point, competitively speaking, had come at the short eleventh, reflected Katie, leaning on her 3-iron and wondering how a strong left to right wind was going to help. The depression, in every sense, which was the left-hand bunker, was the result of a German war time pilot's decision to jettison his last bomb before landing. Veronica's ball plugged into the soft sand under the overhang. When the fourth hack buried it even deeper, she threw down her sand-wedge and burst into tears. Two men were waiting impatiently on the tee so Katie bundled her towards a clump of firs to recover. She finally hiccupped into silence. When she said, 'I've got to tell someone,' Katie propped herself against a convenient trunk and waited for the story of her latest effort to conceive. One couldn't be cruel enough to drag her back to the game before giving a sympathetic ear to what had gone wrong this time. But Veronica was beyond words. She reached into the pocket of her anorak and pulled out an envelope.

The signature on the single sheet of paper was the same. Katie looked at the message and felt sick. 'Did you know your husband has recently had a son by another woman?' She looked at Veronica's tortured face and tried to imagine the agony of knowing somebody else has given your husband what he wanted most in all the world. And for someone who wanted children as desperately as Veronica, this was a mortal blow. Even if the statement were untrue, however convincingly her husband denied it, she would never be quite sure. Veronica, Katie felt, belonged to the no-smoke-without-fire school. This was one marriage which would never be the same again. She wondered if there was a clue in that and then forgot about it.

* * *

It was nearly dusk by the time she got home. Veronica had insisted on finishing the round and had put on a gallant

39

show of normality. Afterwards she had refused a drink and driven away. Katie also avoided the bar, unwilling to face possible questions from the men who had witnessed the episode in the bunker. It was the matter of publicity which had occupied her mind all the way back. Now that a fourth letter had come to light, it was obvious that someone should tell the authorities what was going on. In fact, it should have been done after the receipt of the very first envelope. As wife of the director of an intelligence organisation, Katie knew that very well. If only she had done it with the initial, the innocuous one, the whole business might have been cleared up by now. But she had hesitated, unwilling to instigate an investigation on the strength of one crackpot letter. Now the picture had changed. Now people were being hurt. But wouldn't innocent people, such as Veronica, be even more injured if the affair was made public? And public would be the operative word. No one could call the Military Police unobtrusive. This, she knew, would be the job of the Special Investigations Branch, but what experience did they have of this type of misdemeanour? It wasn't their field at all. The soldiery weren't given to writing poison pen letters. The soldiers, in fact, weren't much given to writing. Police intervention at this stage could mean the irretrievable wreck of more than one marriage. And her own might well be the first.

As she decelerated along Acacia Avenue lights were springing up over front doors and in kitchen windows. Children were coming home from school. Soon would begin the nightly exodus from the Headquarters building. All of us safe in our little boxes, thought Katie. But for how much longer?

4

For as long as he could remember, Rhodri Rees-Williams had wanted to know the reason why. Maybe it was part of his heritage, this passion for knowledge. He was born in the cleverly-converted Welsh farmhouse which was his parents' weekend retreat and his mother's reluctant concession to her husband's nationality. She much preferred the view from Birmingham City Hall. Rhodri and his father, a consultant neurologist, lived for the holidays at Trelleck. Not that there was much to do there, apart from riding and occasional fishing. It was just the fact of being back in Wales. The air was like sparkling wine and, from the top of the house, the eye could follow the line of hills right as far as the Brecon Beacons. There was an enormous smoke-blackened fireplace in the sitting-room but the heart of the house was the rectangular kitchen which had been a byre in the original building. One wall had been replaced by windows over-looking the Wye valley and the rising ground beyond. On the kinder days, it was flooded with morning sunshine. For Rhodri, it was magic.

He went to school in England because it was what his parents wanted. When anyone was unwise enough to abbreviate his name, he insisted on the h in the right place. When he was old enough to insist, he chose the University of Wales instead of Oxford. He spent three years in Cardiff where he took a first in modern languages and played some spectacular rugby. Restless, mercurial, he then experimented with various jobs on the fringes of journalism and big business, but it was finally in a building in one of Whitehall's quieter side-streets that he found what he had been seeking — a challenge. When he was thirty, he met and married Megan.

'What was she like?', Katie had once asked him. Only once because she wasn't sure how much she wanted to know.

'Dark hair, brown eyes, enchanting lilt to her voice. Or so I thought,' said Rhodri with candour, ''till I stopped hearing the voice itself and listened to what it was saying.'

'You mean she was disagreeing with you?'

'Oh, nothing like that.' Rhodri grinned. 'She was intelligent. And shrewd. But no imagination.' At that point Katie had changed the conversation. She wasn't sure how strong she was herself on imagination. But she could guess how Megan must have felt, facing irretrievable breakdown of marriage at the age of twenty-four. According to Rhodri, she had got over it, gone back to studying law and re-married. Some day, Katie thought, she would like to meet Megan. But not yet. Not till she felt safe enough in her marriage to view her predecessor with objectivity.

★　★　★

Katie spent Thursday morning in wholehearted preparation for the morrow. She hoovered and dusted and polished. She cleaned the silver and she made an apple pie. At midday she got out the car and drove round to the BP garage. Gary made such a business of ignoring her that she hastily withdrew and parked on a strip of grass at the side of the maintenance building, carefully lining up the car so that the number-plates couldn't be seen from the road. Then she settled down to wait.

What happened that afternoon was a period of excruciating boredom followed by an unexpected bonus. After the first hour, she found it hard to keep her eyes open. Nothing, literally nothing, had happened. She was surprised the post office managed to stay in business. If she had expected to see a furtive figure — or indeed any figure — pushing up the yellow tin flap of the letter-box, she had to admit she was wrong. In the next hour, she saw a stout German Hausfrau in an unmistakably Teutonic hat and two British N.C.O.s enter the post office and subsequently emerge. She was tired and thirsty and, above all, hungry, thinking longingly of the packet of sandwiches inadvertently left on the kitchen table. It was getting on for closing time when someone, in a manner that really only could be described as furtive, approached the postbox with the yellow lid. It was Margaret Tolworthy. And not long back from golf because she was still wearing slacks. Katie ducked down behind the wheel and watched her push an envelope hastily into the slot. Then she turned and scuttled away. Katie stared at her vanishing figure. What the Brigadier would have thought of such a performance, she couldn't imagine. It was all extremely odd.

Suddenly she noticed a flash of white against the yellow of the box. She got out of the car casually, as though stretching her legs, skirted the traffic at the petrol pumps and strolled over the road. She found she was right. Margaret had been in such a hurry she had dropped the lid on a corner of the envelope. There was no going back now. With one hand Katie grasped the corner, with the other she lifted the lid.

She supposed she had expected the case to be solved on the spot. She could have wept with frustration when she read the address on the envelope. Frau J. Müller, Feldkirchen, Lindenstrasse 57. She dropped it in the box and went back to the car. From the driving seat she saw the German postman come out of the post office and start to clear the box. If anyone received a poison-pen letter tomorrow morning — that is, if any victim admitted getting a letter of this afternoon's date — then she was on the wrong track.

★   ★   ★

If she hadn't been reduced to clutching at straws, Katie would have gone straight home. But she kept thinking of Margaret Tolworthy's uncharacteristic behaviour — and anything out of the ordinary was worth a follow up. Feldkirchen was less than eight kilometres away and she had plenty of petrol . . . Within a quarter of an hour, she was cruising down Lindenstrasse. Number fifty-seven was at the far end. She cut the engine and looked at the house. Like all the others, it was small and square with a first floor balcony and a steep, sloping roof. Unlike all the others, there were no frilled nylon curtains at the windows, no array of pot plants facing the street. Number fifty-five next door, she noted, had pleated and swathed draperies arranged with mathematical precision above a formidable muster of cactus leaves: number fifty-nine had a fine show of cyclamen beneath its quota of net. One thing was clear — it was no German housewife who occupied number fifty-seven. She got out of the car, walked up the short path to the front door and rang the bell. What she would say when it was answered, she had no idea. She could only trust in the inspiration of the moment. As it happened, she didn't immediately have to say anything. A girl with straight reddish hair lowered a child to the floor and held out her hand. 'I'm Jane Tolworthy,' she said. 'I suppose you've come about the letter?'

A couple of minutes later, it had all been sorted out. It wasn't very difficult, Katie realised, once she knew Jane wasn't referring to the letter now nestling cosily in its niche in the German post office. She looked at Jane Tolworthy with interest. So this was the daughter who had been relegated to somewhere nice and far away — like Canada.

'Come in,' said Jane. 'I'm giving Gaby her tea.' Katie sat at the kitchen table with a large cup of coffee and a roll lavishly spread with liver sausage, and listened. 'All this spiel about Frau Müller is for the benefit of the neighbours,' Jane explained. 'The truth is I'm not married and Mama is terrified in case someone finds out and spreads the glad news round the camp. Well, not long ago she got a nasty little note in block capitals — you know the sort of thing? — through her letter box. I burnt it as soon as she showed it to me but you can guess what it said.' She paused a moment. Katie, mouth still full of delicious liver sausage, nodded. 'When I saw your number plate, I thought someone in authority might be investigating.'

'I am investigating,' admitted Katie, 'but not in what you might call a disinterested capacity.' She decided she liked and trusted this girl. 'I'm a victim too, and I stand to lose a lot more than reputation. I suppose you haven't any idea who the writer might be?'

'I honestly can't think. You see, I never go near the camp. I cut myself off entirely when I moved in here with

Hans.' She hoisted her daughter on to her knee. Gaby held a mug of milk in two minute hands and continued to stare with large unblinking blue eyes. 'There's such a big turnover in that place that most of my friends would probably have moved on anyway. The villagers here call me Frau Müller and I let them, chiefly because it's easier than teaching them how to pronounce Tolworthy.'

'I suppose,' Katie hazarded, 'your parents had you slotted for the Guards' Chapel in white organdy with four bridesmaids?'

'You can say that again! From the day of my seventeenth birthday, there they were, a series of selected subalterns. The boredom was mutual.'

'How did you meet Hans?'

'I joined a local ski club. We used to go to the Eifel or the Harz at weekends. You didn't have to be an expert, it was just fun. Hans drove the bus the first time. He's a super skier too. He works in a garage — maybe some day he'll own it.' Her voice was full of pride and confidence.

Poor Margaret, thought Katie; longing for a presentable son-in-law, concealing the shameful reality of a daughter living with a German garage mechanic. But her sympathies were with the daughter. Jane must have sensed that, because she said impulsively she hoped they would meet again.

'I said before that I couldn't think who could be writing those letters,' she went on, 'but I've just had a rather horrible idea — now that I know other people are suffering. Could it possibly be Mother herself? Maybe she's mentally disturbed. You see, she's torn both ways now. She adores Gaby, but tradition and upbringing — and Father — make it impossible for her to come to terms with my living in sin, as she still calls it, poor dear. And she could have written the letter — the one she showed me — to herself, just as a blind,' Jane concluded unhappily.

It was quite dark by the time Katie

got back to Niederdorf. Her timetable for the evening centred exclusively on bath and early bed, she slid the car up the ramp into the garage. Only then did she notice the lights in the downstairs windows. There was but one explanation. Rhodri was home again. The front door opened before she reached it.

'Katie! What the hell is going on?'

5

Katie walked slowly across the small patch of lawn outside the kitchen window. Her only coherent thought was how differently she had planned for his return; the food, the flowers, the loving welcome. She wasn't even wearing any lipstick, her hair was swept into tangles, her old anorak hung from her shoulders. Worse was to come — much worse. As soon as she moved into the hall, she saw the letter on the table. It was addressed in block capitals.

She couldn't open it, she couldn't even pick it up. She did the only sensible thing — she ignored it.

'I'm sorry, darling,' she said contritely, and moved past him into the sitting-room. As she had intended, he followed her. The standard lamp gave a muted glow, almost like twilight after the harsh glare of the overhead light in the hall. She put her arms round his neck and buried her face in his shoulder. Rhodri hugged her close.

'Of course!' he exclaimed. 'I should have remembered. Golf day, isn't it? Did you play all afternoon as well? I couldn't understand it when nobody answered the phone.' Katie's hesitation was momentary. Rhodri hardly knew her golfing friends and was most unlikely to come across anyone who would mention her absence. Imperceptibly she relaxed. 'I even look like a lady golfer,' she murmured. She inhaled the comforting blend of tobacco and after-shave. 'You weren't supposed to come back till to-morrow.'

'I know. We finished earlier than expected and an intrepid birdman gave me a lift back in his machine.'

Rhodri, as always, after a period of intense concentration, expected her to be at home when he returned, giving him warmth and laughter, helping him unwind.

'I've made you a luscious apple pie,'

she said softly. 'Tell you what — I'll run you a bath while you have a drink and read your mail and then . . . '

'There was a letter for you,' Rhodri said, kissing her lightly, gratefully accepting normality.

'Probably an advertisement. I've had them before. I'll get you some ice . . . ' Rhodri was already in the study, pouring himself a whisky. Katie removed the envelope, thrust it into her handbag and went into the kitchen.

She felt no elation at the ease with which she had misled her husband. It was the first time she had consciously deceived him. By that small betrayal, she had made a dent in the armour of their unity. Was that how it had started with Claire? Or Veronica?

When Rhodri was in the bath, singing as all Welshmen are supposed to sing, Katie sat at her dressing-table and tore open the unstamped envelope. Better to get it over with now while she still had time to compose herself for the rest of the evening. Rhodri was unusually perceptive. Unless preoccupied with some aspect of his job, he nearly always knew when she was worried or unwell and trying to hide it from him. She had been lucky so far. How long could she keep it up?

This time the message seemed to be as innocuous as the first one. But there was a sting in the tail. 'Nobody likes spies,' it read. 'Especially your husband.' It was quite true. If she had to err, he would have preferred adultery on a thumping scale. Meanness of spirit, to Rhodri, was the cardinal sin, and snooping certainly came under that heading. She could protest, of course, even justify her action. But whatever the outcome, things would never be the same again.

Even now she didn't know why she had done it. It had been an impulse, born of a sudden unease. Rhodri was often called out unexpectedly; usually the phone would ring and he'd answer it, say something like 'Urgent signal, see you later' and off he'd go. But that time it had been different. The telephone had rung, yes, but she had been nearby and she could have sworn that no one had spoken at the other end . . .

She brushed her hair and plaited it in a pigtail, put on a velvet housecoat, renewed her lipstick.

'That's my girl!' said Rhodri. 'When do we eat?'

★ ★ ★

Claire Fordyn was resignedly laying the table for six. Until recently she had cooked for Barney, when he returned from school, a meal she hoped would comprise tea, supper and hearty bed-time snack. But an ever-increasing reluctance to face a monosyllabic Mark across an expanse of dinner table had led to their son being allowed to do his homework first and join them at seven-thirty. Barney was a major complication to any meal but especially at weekends when you added his vast appetite to his habitual unpunctuality and the presence of three or four uninvited — and hungry — friends. Even without the extra mouths, Claire thought helplessly, the new arrangement didn't benefit the larder or shorten the working day because it just meant that he expected tea before and bedtime snack afterwards as a matter of course. She thought briefly and enviously of Katie, just up the road, cool and glamorous, probably having a leisurely pre-dinner drink with that attractive and enigmatic husband of hers. Had she and Mark once looked like that, in Camberley or Catterick, to couples for whom the foundations had already been eroded by human changeability? Oh well, Katie would probably have children, Rhodri would have to adapt . . . Resolutely she went back to the kitchen and took the casserole out of the oven.

Mark usually made an effort with Barney's friends — not least, Claire suspected, because of his personal image as a father. But also, in an odd way, to sublimate his deep disappointment when Barney had failed to pass his public school entrance examination. Not the academic type, Mark had declared to his contemporaries whose well-mannered and sleekly uniformed children flew out from England three times a year. More of an individualist, he would add, throwing the latest Army school report into the wastepaper basket. There had been hopes of exceptional linguistic ability till it transpired that Barney's ungrammatical but fast and idiomatic German had been picked up merely for exchanging insults with the natives. Apparently self-sufficient, Barney Fordyn went his own way.

Lindy had turned up this evening and she always made things easier in that her ideas were seldom conventional.

'How's it been this term?' Mark asked her, passing the potatoes.

'Boring,' said Lindy. When she joined the top class, she had been disliked and resented by the other girls, all of them at least two years older. She knew that being prettier than most of them hadn't helped either. Large green eyes looked out from under blonde-streaked brown hair cut like a mop. 'I think traditional education is superfluous these days, don't you?' she added. Barney and two younger boys who had apparently wandered in from the street stopped eating long enough to voice their approval. 'For girls,' Lindy ended.

'Is this a sort of inverted Women's Lib?' asked Mark, amused. His eyes met Claire's reminiscently. She had once been a fierce and, to him, delightfully naïve protagonist of women's rights. Inappropriately he was reminded of someone instinctively happy to be a woman in a man's world. Joanna . . . His eyes dropped. He concentrated without appetite on the passage of fork to mouth. Conversation flowed spasmodically round the table. Claire brought in a large treacle tart. Barney demolished his share and announced that he and Lindy were going to the cinema.

'Presumably you've done your home-work,' said Claire. Heaven knows he'd been upstairs long enough. Barney decided sensibly that this was not a misconception that need be denied. 'Come on, Lindy. Got any money?'

'You know I haven't. I spent all of the far-from-generous on Monday.'

'Dad?' Barney waited expectantly. Mark came back from a long way off and produced his wallet. When they had all gone, he went into the study and poured himself a stiff whisky. What on earth was he going to do?

★　★　★

He didn't have to come to a decision. Joanna killed herself on Monday morning. It isn't easy to find a suitable place for hanging oneself in an Army quarter but she'd managed it. She was small and slim and didn't put too much strain on the overhead light fitting in the hall. She had knotted the washing-line round her neck and kicked away the chair.

Claire wouldn't have heard the news so soon if she hadn't happened to telephone, just after breakfast, an acquaintance who lived in the same road as the dead girl and who, shocked and appalled, was only too ready to pass on such details as had come her way. Colin had found his wife's body when he went downstairs in search of an unexpected cup of tea. He had taken painkillers the night before because of toothache, and must have been sleeping heavily when Joanna left his side. Medical opinion put her death between five and six a.m. She hadn't left a note. They'd seemed such a happy couple, no one could understand it.

Joanna hadn't understood it herself. She hadn't even tried to put it into words. What she knew was that she couldn't bear for Colin, who loved her and was so good to her, to find out about Mark. If she wasn't there, there

wouldn't be another anonymous letter.
It was as easy as that. She couldn't run
away because she hadn't any money,
except what Colin gave her, and
nowhere to go. Her parents had died in
a car crash and her elder sister was
married to a man with hot hands and a
long reach. No, Ellen certainly wouldn't
want her around. She didn't stop to
consider that Colin might forgive her
and understand, whatever the scandal:
that he might prefer to have her at any
cost. She didn't reason at all. She just
took what was, for her, the only way
out.

6

It was the suicide that rushed Katie into hasty and unpopular action. There was no proof that Joanna had received a poison pen letter but everything pointed that way. Katie had met Joanna, an ineffective yet endearing beginner, at the Golf Club and had a drink with her a couple of times. She, like Claire, heard the news via the telephone. She leant against the wall, sick at heart, thinking of that slender childish neck cruelly encircled by a tightening length of nylon cord. The picture was all too vivid. She wrenched her mind away from the bleak cold hours before dawn and concentrated on the question of what was to be done.

She didn't ring Claire, she just went along. Without comment Claire produced coffee and, as an afterthought, the brandy decanter. They sat at the kitchen table.

'I know we're in the same boat,' said Katie. Claire didn't pretend to misunderstand. 'Joanna must have got a letter too,' Katie continued. 'It's too much of a coincidence that she should take her own life at this particular time. What are we going to do?'

A good measure of brandy had brought the colour back to Claire's face and authority to her voice. 'One thing we aren't going to do', she stated flatly, 'is tell the military police. Apart from our own problems, investigation would unearth whatever Joanna killed herself to hide. Don't we owe it to Colin to keep it a secret?'

'It isn't a secret any more,' Katie pointed out. 'Somebody in this camp knows. The point is that there's a reasonable certainty Joanna has died as a direct result of some busybody's pen.'

'There's no proof she ever got a letter.' Claire was being obstinate. Heaven knows, Katie thought, she herself didn't want an investigation either. But she couldn't get rid of a burden of responsibility. If she had reported the very first letter, maybe Joanna would still be alive. 'Alright, then. No police,' she conceded. 'That means we've got to do the work ourselves. The first essential is the pooling of information: only that way can we get an idea of who could know so much about our private lives.' Katie hoped she sounded impressive. Claire didn't look happy but she had to agree. This was no time for hugging one's own precarious secrets. 'Who else?' she asked. 'Veronica for one. And Margaret Tolworthy. We'd better get hold of them now.'

Half an hour later, action had moved to the dining-room. Six letters lay on the table, three of Katie's and one each belonging to the others. All except the two latest had been received on a Friday morning. The various messages were absorbed without comment, though the implication of Mark Fordyn's alleged affaire caused raised eyebrows and an uncomfortable silence. Margaret Tolworthy, stiffly disapproving, said she had no idea how anyone could have found out about her daughter. She managed to infer it was no damn business of anyone else's anyway. Veronica, head in the sand as usual, muttered to the effect there was no proof her husband had ever strayed from the conjugal bed.

'Don't be stupid,' said Katie, unwisely. 'It's only too clear that, as far as authenticity goes, whoever writes these letters has done her homework.' That fixed any last hope of mutual understanding. Not only was she the youngest member present, she was also the only non-Army wife. Watching the others gradually — and verbosely — putting up the shutters, she came to the inescapable conclusion that she was the one person interested in discovering the identity of the writer.

'If the police are brought in, I shall,

of course, deny any knowledge of the whole business,' stated Margaret Tolworthy. Neither Claire nor Veronica dissociated themselves from such an obviously face-saving course.

Their expressions varied from the unyielding to the obstinate to the evasive. Looking at them, Katie had a sudden and quite unreasonable hunch. It wasn't just because of lack of co-operation. Somebody was covering up. One of the women at this table had written the poison-pen letters.

★   ★   ★

There was no point in staying any longer. Katie retrieved her letters, refused a half-hearted offer of fresh coffee and let herself out into the windy morning. She walked fast up the road, head down, thinking hard. Once in the privacy of number thirteen, she went straight to the telephone. Advice she must have, and there was only one person to whom she could turn.

Patrick St. Clair Darran was that anachronism in the present day army — a loner. In his view, the most exciting places in peacetime were those forbidden to wives and families. And Patrick had to be where the action was. One was posted, occasionally, to places like Niederdorf but sometimes one had to take the smooth with the rough. In due course he would leave for, he hoped, some distant danger spot where professional expertise and the ability to survive occupied most of one's waking days. He had once wanted to marry, long years ago, but at that particular time it had been impossible. And so he had channelled all his energies into soldiering. So far, it had been enough . . . He was studying plans for a NATO exercise when the telephone rang. 'Patrick? It's Katie. I want to talk to you about something rather urgently. Are you very busy?'

'D'you mean today? How about this evening?'

'Preferably outside the camp,' said

Katie. One thing she could certainly do without was an anonymous letter implicating Patrick. 'Tell you what. I'm free most of Wednesday. How about a boat on the Rhein?'

'Can Rhodri spare you?'.

'Easily.' She laughed. 'He likes lunching at the Officers' Club. There's a choice of menu.'

'It'll mean an early start,' warned Patrick, 'if you want to take in the most dramatic part of the river.'

'Dawn?'

'Dawn it is.'

★ ★ ★

When she had washed the breakfast dishes, made the bed and flicked a duster over the more obvious surfaces, Katie went for a walk in the woods to consider the situation. She hadn't gone more than a hundred yards before she realised that the odds against Margaret Tolworthy had shortened appreciably in the last few days. In fact, there were two points which definitely put her in the running for favourite. The most important was the time of her arrival at Claire's party. Patrick had been one of the last and Margaret, according to Claire, had come in after him. Barney's parting sentence that evening was clear in her mind. He'd been talking about the letter and he'd said, 'It wasn't there when Colonel Darran left the bottle of wine on the hall table.' Had anyone else entered the house after the Tolworthys? It didn't seem likely.

The second indication was a plausible reason for frequent use of the German post office which was the clearing station only for local and other continental letters. If suspicion eventually should centre on those who had actually been seen to push letters into the yellow box, she had an innocent explanation. As a postscript, there was Jane Tolworthy's reluctantly expressed fear that her mother might be mentally disturbed. It all added up. And yet . . . Katie still wasn't convinced. She could visualise a sudden brainstorm but not a sustained campaign. Also — and here was a real stumbling block — how would Margaret have known about the rendezvous in the woods? It was laughable to suggest that Margaret could have been following Katie who was shadowing Rhodri . . . Or was it? Katie realised that instinctively her feet this morning were taking the same path they had trodden that summer evening. Once again she was walking through the firs, her footsteps soft on a carpet of needles. But this time she was looking to right and left. And not more than a hundred yards away to the left she could glimpse the outlines of a row of houses. The well-remembered plan of the camp superimposed itself on the muted greens and bronzes of this part of the forest. Over there was the street familiarly known as Brigadier's Row. Over there, not a stone's-throw away, was the house in which Margaret Tolworthy lived.

For a long time Katie stood there, listening to the soughing of the wind in the treetops. She was thinking that Margaret almost certainly had the local knowledge on which to base a series of anonymous letters. She would have known about Veronica's problems from long hours on the golf course: she could have guessed what Mark was up to through friendship with Claire. And it wasn't outside the bounds of possibility that she had seen, from the spacious patio, maybe, or while in the trimly manicured garden, two people she recognised . . . And that, decided Katie, suddenly resolute, was one thing on which she could check.

There was a small iron gate let into the hedge which divided the woods from the garden. Katie stood with her hand on the latch, eyes carefully scanning the south-facing windows. There was a fitful sun playing tricks with the shadows cast by the trees behind her. A curtain twitched at one of the upstairs windows: was it moved by a hand or just a wayward breeze? Katie stepped into the garden. As she turned to close the gate, she found that she was looking straight down the glade to the path she had been following. The sun disappeared behind a black-edged cloud. The quality of menace inherent in any German landscape shrouded the encroaching forest. It was with no surprise that she heard the voice from the patio behind her. Come into my parlour, said the spider to the fly.

It was a very tasteful parlour. By skilful arrangement, attention was focussed on personal possessions rather than quartermaster's G-plan. There was a collection of what looked like Meissen in a wall cabinet, an inlaid work-box beside one of the armchairs and a couple of piecrust tables. On the mantelpiece there were two framed photographs. One of them pictured a good-looking boy, the other a girl with straight reddish hair and blue eyes. 'Jane!' said Katie involuntarily and with pleasure. And instantly regretted it.

'Where did you meet my daughter?' asked Margaret gently.

There were only two ways of dealing with a question like that. One was the truth which, in the circumstances, was inadvisable. It was also unfair to Jane who would almost certainly be catechised by her mother. The other tactic was prevarication. Katie realised sadly that she was becoming rather good at prevarication.

'If that is your son,' she answered, 'this can only be your daughter. Besides, she looks like you. I think it's the way she holds her head.' Unknowingly, she had hit on the one trait that went straight to Margaret's heart. Unable to trace her own patrician features in either of her children, she had long ago settled for a resemblance in carriage. She unbent, noticeably.

'Would you like a drink? I usually have a glass of sherry before lunch.'

After all the crises of the morning, Katie could have done with something considerably stronger. But she was lucky to be offered anything at all.

'Thank you,' she said. 'I'd like that.'

Watching her face as she poured from a cut-glass decanter, Katie tried to imagine Margaret Tolworthy sitting, maybe in this room, at that desk, cutting words from newspapers, glueing them together, printing block capitals on a plain white envelope. Such abnormality seemed completely out of place in an ordered ambience like this. When, a quarter of an hour later, the Brigadier bustled in, shook hands, praised a recent job done by Rhodri's department, offered to have her driven home, the image receded even further. That sort of thing just didn't happen in this sort of household. Katie, back in her own kitchen, breaking eggs for omelettes, admitted to herself that opportunity and alleged instability were not enough. Actually to write poison-pen letters, there had to be a motive, an animosity against society as a whole or directed at a certain group of people. Margaret Tolworthy did not seem to fit into either category.

7

Patrick had not exaggerated. Embarking at Bingen, Katie looked back at the wide tranquil river flowing between low banks and round wooded islands. Standing in the bows of the 'Regenbogen', the view was entirely different. One saw only that two mountain masses had drawn closer together until they presented an almost unbroken rock wall. The opposing cliffs seemed a handsbreadth apart, the current raced fast and smooth, the crags shut out the sky. Katie stood spellbound, hands grasping the rail, mesmerised by the gap ahead. Impossible that so much water could be contained in a ravine so narrow. Suddenly the cliffs were towering on either side and the Rhein poured swiftly and powerfully into the gorge. The channel widened. A small town appeared at the water's edge, huddled at the foot of a precipice crowned by a ruined castle. Around the next bend of the river, another village sparkled in the morning sunshine, its red-tiled roofs rising to the dark green of vineyards and on up to the spectacular wreck of a Gothic citadel. Patrick, fair hair blown back from his forehead, pointed out the route on the map.

'Bingen, Boppard and Bacharach . . . Sounds like a slightly shady firm of solicitors,' he remarked.

'Or a team of song writers,' said Katie and giggled. All at once she felt free — far away from the stultifying atmosphere, the gossip, the pettiness which characterised any enclosed community. It was partly the sheer Teutonic extravagance of the gorge, partly the undemanding company of someone known since childhood. It was irresponsibility, immunity, a day at the circus . . .

They had coffee and fresh-baked rolls and black cherry jam in the glass-enclosed restaurant, and round each bend saw a new enchantment like a series of coloured slides, each one perfect in itself. They were standing once more by the rail when the Lorelei Rock, steep and craggy, swept into view by the small town of St. Goar. Katie watched it approach, her mind full of the legend. She turned her head towards Patrick and he looked back at her. For one dizzy second, he was a reckless sailor and she the siren with long drenched hair and smiling lips, luring him into the treacherous waters which swirled, round the reefs. She blinked and he was real again, son of an impecunious landowner, the quiet little boy who could be so surprisingly tough, now the seasoned veteran of a dozen campaigns.

'I've never thanked you properly for the bottle of wine,' she said.

'Now that you mention it, what a very good idea!'

They sat inside again, sipping cold dry Rheinpfalz. Clouds were blowing over the sun, the late-October chill suddenly presaged the snows of winter.

The tourist season was long over, the boat comparatively empty. There was no one near enough to hear what they were saying.

'I'm going to tell you a story,' began Katie . . .

★　★　★

The shadows were lengthening when the '*Regenbogen*' burst triumphantly out of the gorge at Koblenz, and the lights of Köln were shimmering on the water when finally they disembarked. They had talked, lunched, paced the deck, intent on the matter in hand yet always aware of the world slipping past the streamlined bows. Katie had mentioned no names and stuck as far as possible to what facts she knew. Patrick's immediate advice was, as she had known it must be, to turn the whole business over to the police. 'That's what I wanted to do. But it's no good, Patrick — the others will deny they ever received a letter, and that just leaves someone writing silly messages to me. They couldn't even be called threatening, so what would there be to investigate?' Patrick lit a cigarette and pushed away his coffee-cup.

'I, unlike you, would have no alternative. I would have to report it.' His wide mouth was set in a straight line, his eyebrows — darker than his hair — drawn together, blue-grey eyes intent and alert. He looked what he was, a formidable opponent. 'From what I know about the anonymous letter disease, it stems from two main causes. Number one is motivated, i.e. the working out of a grudge, and is directed against one person or a group of people. Number two is general rather than particular: that means that the writer is apt to be indiscriminate in her choice of victim and has chosen this method of working off the unhappiness and frustration in her own life. I say 'her' because poison-pen letters are rarely written by men.'

'Into which category would you put these?'

'Definitely the first. The sex motive is there, as it always is, but, from what you've quoted, it is unobtrusive. And there's no obscene language which is one of the hallmarks of the second category.' He ground out his cigarette. 'I take it that recipients and suspects all belong to a certain set?' Katie nodded. She wasn't going to mention the Golf Club. She didn't want him, however unintentionally, superimposing faces on shadowy outlines.

'You're determined to go it alone?' he asked a bit later. Katie nodded again. 'I'm the only one I can trust.'

'Well, look out for the little things. Not so much cigarette ash or a lipstick's trace, but a look, a gesture, an unexpected action . . . ' He didn't smile. 'And, Katie — take care.'

★ ★ ★

'I missed you,' said Rhodri abruptly. He put his arms round her. 'It wasn't a very good lunch either. No good having a choice if you don't like any of them.' He tilted her head so that he could see her face. 'Don't go away again.'

'I won't,' promised Katie, thankful to be able to guarantee physical nearness, at the same time profoundly grateful that he didn't know the other self, the one so unlike the Katie who talked and laughed and cooked and said good-night. When finally she drifted into sleep, her head on his shoulder, she dreamt of three water-nymphs beneath the dark rippling waves, and their names were Bingen and Boppard and Bacharach . . .

Next day was Thursday which was the day, she hoped, that Gary would be making some effort to earn his retainer. Five-thirty wasn't a good time as traffic was heavy but she managed to attract his attention long enough to check the tyres. The afternoon's bag, she learnt, was not exceptional: they had all been there before. It included three school-girls, Margaret Tolworthy (presumably another letter to her daughter), Barney Fordyn (whom Gary had known at school) and the ubiquitous German Frau with the pudding-basin hat. Katie told him she was taking him off the payroll for the moment and he reminded her she owed him five marks. As business transactions went, reflected Katie, this one lacked most things including dividends. It was a long time before she realised that the employer should have taken the trouble to check on the staff-work.

On Friday morning, Rhodri seemed in no hurry to set off for his office. He mislaid a favourite tie, had a long telephone conversation and asked for a third cup of coffee. Katie, gently urging him towards the door, was the first to hear the distinctive stutter of the German postman's moped. It slowed down as it always did because the house was on a corner. But it didn't accelerate round the bend. It stopped. There was a brief pause, then footsteps rang out on the path.

'Good!' said Rhodri cheerfully. 'Something for us.'

★ ★ ★

It had been one of Katie's nightmares that some day an anonymous letter would drop onto the mat when both she and Rhodri were in the hall. That fear had been intensified since the evening he had returned unexpectedly early from Berlin and actually found one of them. On that occasion she had had time to invent an explanation and to present it casually, as if the whole thing had no importance. What was more, he had obviously accepted that there was advertising material in the envelope. As it happened, firms selling insurance or owners of new restaurants in the district frequently did advertise in this way. This time, however, there was a difference. If it was addressed to her, Rhodri would expect her to open it on the spot as if it were a Christmas card. He would be surprised and hurt if she refused. What was more, if it were addressed in capital letters he would remember the other one. Katie, mesmerised, stared at the flap through which the letter must come.

The young postman was conscientious. He liked his job and his shiny new bike and he meant to make no mistakes. He glanced at the address again and found that the badly-written number was 15 and not 13 as he had supposed. Whistling, he retreated down the path. Rhodri turned to pick up his briefcase. 'Whatever's the matter, darling? You're shaking!'

Katie leant back against the wall. 'I thought it might be a — a bomb', she said weakly.

'Well, I was here, wasn't I? I'd have picked it up. I know how to deal with things like that.' When he had gone, Katie realised that those words would have been equally applicable if he had picked up a poison-pen letter.

Sitting on the stairs, chin on knees, she found she was thinking more clearly than she had for some time. For example, what was the use of finding out who had posted letters yesterday afternoon when she had no means of knowing if one — or more than one — was being delivered in the camp this morning? It was putting the cart before the horse. That sort of playing-at-detectives wasn't going to get her anywhere. If she was still convinced that one of those present at the meeting in Claire's house had written the letters, then all she could usefully do at the moment was to eliminate the least likely. Margaret Tolworthy, by reason of character and background, was now reduced to a question mark. Possible but improbable. So how about Veronica?

One thing immediately sprang to mind about Veronica. Slowly Katie sat upright. If anyone had a grudge, even a supposed grudge, it had to be Veronica. Katie had seen her look at other people's children and had been sorry for her in an irritated way because she did make such a parade of her neurosis. She couldn't do anything about the children, but she could work off her frustration by making their mothers miserable. That certainly applied to Margaret and Claire. But how about herself? She and Rhodri had decided not to start a family till they returned to England and their own home. But of course! Katie nearly fell off her stair in her excitement. Herself most of all — because she presumably could have a child and didn't. That, in Veronica's eyes, was the ultimate sin, the unforgivable insult. That was probably why she'd had more letters than anyone else. Then, of course, Veronica had sent one to herself as a blind. Katie got up and went through to the kitchen, Veronica's face floating through her mind. That was when the theory came to an abrupt end. Veronica's face, as remembered in a copse just off the eleventh green at Tolrath, had expressed what was surely genuine agony. If she had to write to herself a letter she might have to show to other people, why did she have to be so specific? Deflated, Katie made another cup of coffee. After that she decided she might as well go and call on Veronica anyway. Seeing a woman in her own environment could influence one's judgment. It had swung the balance in Margaret's favour. Could it be a factor in eliminating Veronica?

★ ★ ★

Veronica Caldicott was not a natural home-maker. The only furniture she really wanted were cots and high chairs. In her view, the recess in the hall had been expressly designed for the parking of prams. Denied this outlet, she just didn't bother. What the army provided was functional, and could from any other point of view be ignored. The fact that the carpet clashed with the chair-covers and that neither complemented the curtains had never occurred to her. Nor had the idea of applying for exchanges. John never noticed his surroundings, she would say with some complacency, so why worry?

The hospital with its staff quarters was situated a couple of miles outside the camp, just off the road to the golf course. The Caldicotts' house was semi-detached but with a large back garden overlooking open country. Veronica was not expecting visitors nor, was her unspoken comment, did she want any.

'I won't stay long,' said Katie, smiling brightly, 'but I just happened to be passing your door . . . ' Reluctantly Veronica led the way into the sitting-room. Katie glanced around, taking in an undistinguished water-colour, two silver cups, a stack of what looked like medical journals in a bookcase.

'I was going to make coffee. You might as well have a cup too,' Veronica said ungraciously and went into the kitchen. Katie moved round the living-room, wondering how two people could make so little impact, thinking that she was wasting her time, sure that she didn't want any more coffee. There wasn't even a newspaper in sight. Bending over a chair to study the titles of half a dozen paperbacks in the bookcase, she inadvertently knocked against the journals. Two of them toppled over, and something which looked like a theatre programme slid to the floor. Katie picked it up. It *was* a theatre programme of seven years previously. She remembered the Oxford Theatre in Shaftesbury Avenue though she had a feeling it was no longer being used as such. She looked at the first page. There was a star who had since gone to America, and five other players. One of them was immediately recognisable. Veronica Maybury, she read, as Hermione. In the accompanying photograph, there she was, squarecut fringe, broad hips, aggressive pose — exactly as she had looked when she opened the front door not five minutes ago. Carefully Katie put the programme back on the shelf and stationed herself at the french windows, gazing absorbedly at a border of desiccated Michaelmas daisies. What price now that tortured expression? Once an actress, always an actress.

8

Veronica seemed to be taking a lot longer than was necessary to open a jar of NAAFI instant coffee. Katie drifted towards the door. Maybe Veronica was thinking up some sort of ploy. Some piece of theatrical skulduggery? Suppose she knew what Katie suspected, what would she do about it? Put something in the coffee? After all, her husband was a doctor, she'd probably know a bit about drugs . . . Gently, Katie opened the door. There was a murmur of voices coming from the kitchen. Katie heard a couple of phrases and relaxed. So that was it: Veronica's *Putzfrau* was on the point of leaving. The conversation indicated a compromise between Veronica's German and the cleaning-woman's English, i.e. mostly English. With a last '*Auf-Wiedersehen*' from Veronica and an unexpected 'Cheery-Bye' in response, the back door closed. Katie, from where she stood, could see a slice of the kitchen which included part of the window. She was just turning away when the woman passed by outside. She only got a quick glimpse of a round face and an ample figure. The overcoat was nondescript. But there was no mistaking that hat.

One of the obstacles, Katie reflected, driving back to the camp, had been the lack of any report on Veronica's presence at the *Postamt*. She lived some distance away, there were other German post offices nearer than Niederdorf. But what could be easier than to ask the woman who worked, as Veronica had admitted, in the camp every afternoon, to mail a letter for her from time to time? The hat wasn't just any old hat. Katie remembered it clearly from her vigil because she'd had little else to look at, all that long afternoon. It was the usual beige velour with a high crown and very little brim but this one had an incongruous bunch of violets emerging cautiously just over the left ear.

Accelerating along the three-lane stretch of road, Katie firmly disposed of the other obstacle. It was partly because of the comfortless house, the large mugs of tepid coffee, above all Veronica's own attitude. Everything pointed to masochism. What followed was that, if Veronica should write a poison-pen letter to herself, she would create a situation most calculated to hurt. The only thing left to do, thought Katie, manoeuvring the car into the garage, was to find a reasonable answer to the question of how Veronica had assembled her material. How, for example, had she found out about Jane Tolworthy? The only person who might know the answer to that one was Jane.

* * *

Rhodri needed the car that afternoon — and then there was the weekend with dinner at the Officers' Club on Saturday and pre-lunch drinks with one of his colleagues on Sunday. It was the following Tuesday before Katie was able to drive out once more to Feldkirchen. November had come in wet and cold: rain fell steadily from a solid grey blanket of sky. Katie shivered and switched on the heater. If one were living in, say, Austria, rain in late autumn would be transformed by the happy certainty that the first snow would be falling on the high peaks not all that far away. Here, the great West German plain stretched its grim uniformity in every direction. Jane Tolworthy's kitchen was an oasis of warmth and security. Whatever their problems, one felt that she and Hans and Gaby had a rare sufficiency. Jane produced a bottle of schnapps and two tiny glasses. 'Down in one,' she instructed, 'that's the way to drink it.' 'Whacko!' said Katie happily. 'All last week I was awash with coffee. The last person who offered me a drink was your mother. Oh it's alright, I didn't tell her I knew you. But after what you said, I did think seriously about her being the author of the anonymous letters.' She didn't say how nearly she had been convinced. 'But I'm practically certain now that there's nothing for you to worry about.'

'Thank heaven for that,' said Jane. 'It's bad enough being a problem child without having a problem parent as well. Let's drink to that.'

'Cheers!' responded Katie and was instantly reminded of Veronica's *Putzfrau*.

'I suppose,' she said slowly, 'you didn't have Gaby at the Army hospital?'

'No way!' Jane laughed. 'That really would have blown it. No — there's a very good local clinic and some of the nurses speak English.' That looked like the end of another promising lead. Katie persisted. 'You had no communication with them at all?'

'Well, once I thought I was going to miscarry and I got in a panic. Hans was away and my German wasn't good enough to explain to his doctor. So I did phone to ask for advice.'

'Who did you talk to?'

'The gynaecologist, of course,' said Jane.

⋆　⋆　⋆

This, then, was how a detective felt when, after weeks of patient plodding, he caught the first heady whiff of the chase: the intoxicating moment when the face of the hunted began to take shape. There were still some questions to answer, some points to be investigated but at last a coherent picture was beginning to form. Katie drove home with the confident feeling that the end was in sight. What she would do with the assembled information she didn't yet know. It was not her province to sit in judgment: all she wanted was to ensure that whoever was responsible should be stopped forthwith.

Now that luck was running her way,

another little piece slipped into place. A vague memory from those countless golf-course conversations came back to her. Hadn't Veronica once mentioned that her husband was a jogger? John didn't play ball games and he didn't like walking, so most mornings and on summer evenings he trundled along the lanes or through the woods. Two or three miles was nothing to someone who enjoyed jogging. It was definitely possible that he had been on the outskirts of the camp, witnessed the unusual sight of wife following husband and subsequently told Veronica about it. He would never have known it was just another little item to be filed away ... As for the assumed triangle involving Claire, Mark and Joanna, the merest hint of gossip would have been enough to set the poison pen in motion.

Oh yes, it all fitted in.

★ ★ ★

The let-down, when it came, was all the more crushing. Especially after such a lovely evening. Rhodri, infected by Katie's gaiety, lit a fire of aromatic pine logs and opened another bottle of wine. They dined by candle-glow and danced by the light of the flickering flames. Next morning Katie woke up in the cold grey dawn and was faced by the one counterblow which could bring her newly-built house of cards tumbling to the ground. The question was there, ready-made, the moment she opened her eyes. What about the letter left on the hall table in Claire Fordyn's house?

The Caldicotts had not been at the party. Veronica wasn't a friend, just a golfing acquaintance, and the Fordyns probably didn't even know her husband. The envelope left on the table that evening had been placed there by hand, according to Barney, who swore that nothing had been pushed through the letter-box. Logic reasserted its inevitable claim. If Veronica had not been among the guests, Veronica had not written the letters. One thing a poison pen does not do and that is publicize her hobby. She certainly doesn't ask another person to convey an envelope addressed in block capitals to someone else's house.

Rhodri slept on. Katie slid out of bed, pulled on her primrose yellow dressing-gown and went downstairs. Dispassionately she looked at last night's débris: the ash in the fireplace, the glasses, a scatter of wax on the dining-room table. She had been so sure, last night, that the end was in sight, that all she had to do was type out her conclusions, present a copy to Veronica and tell her that the original would be held as surety. Shuddering at the thought of the penalties incurred for false accusation, she went into the kitchen and plugged in the kettle. Wrapping her cold hands round a cup of steaming tea, she forced herself to consider the only alternative to Veronica. Claire.

Claire Fordyn was standing in an identical kitchen, looking out at the same view, drawing the same momentary comfort from a cup of hot tea. Jealousy, she now knew, didn't die with its object. Death made no difference. If Joanna had stayed alive, Mark's love for her would probably have lost that overwhelming feeling of rediscovery. As time went by, a major irritation or an accumulation of minor ones — could that little girl voice have begun to grate the teeniest bit? — might have disillusioned him. But now she was preserved in his memory, forever young, the unattainable dream; never to burn the sausages and nag about school bills and grow ungracefully old. And there was nothing that she, Mark's wife, could do about it.

Even to mention her name would lead to recriminations and, inevitably, the charge of speaking ill of the dead. Now that it was too late. Claire saw that her policy had been disastrously wrong. Whatever had deceived her into believing that she would win her husband back by being her usual tolerant, good-humoured and efficient self? That he would come thankfully back to a well-run house and a comforting shoulder? She knew Mark, she'd been married to him for eighteen years. He didn't want an understanding smile, he wanted a hurt and angry wife who would present him with a choice; he desperately needed an opportunity to explain. Not in the early stages, of course, but latterly one flaming row would have cleared the air and led to eventual reconciliation. If only she'd used her head. If only . . . A sudden shower spattered the window-panes. A door opened upstairs. A tap was turned on. There was Barney to chivvy, breakfast to cook, another day to be endured. At eight o'clock attractive, calm, good-natured Claire Fordyn sat down to breakfast with her husband and son. It took all her self-control not to fling her perfectly-scrambled eggs at their uncaring faces.

That evening she had a row with Barney. She had the grace to admit it wasn't really his fault. He had been no more unpredictable or lazy or forgetful than usual; it was just that now she noticed things she had happily let slide before. He had been in the kitchen with Lindy when Rhodri Rees-Williams walked past the window. Rhodri turned his head. He looked amused, interested: there was vitality in his every move.

'Dishy, isn't he?' murmured Lindy, glancing sideways at Barney.

'Not my type,' said Barney, turning her round to face him, 'but you are.' Claire, coming into the room, was reminded vividly and painfully of Mark as he had been when they first met.

'Barney!' she said sharply. 'If you've quite finished fooling around in here, it's time you got on with your homework.' Barney was largely impervious to reprimand. But this was the first time he'd been bawled out in front of

Lindy. He kept his hands on her shoulders and, over her bright head, looked at his mother.

'When — or whether — I decide to do some work is my business.' Lindy, sensing what was coming, slid out of his grasp and made her escape by the back door. With any luck she might catch up with Mr. Rees-Williams . . . Barney didn't move.

'You've got no ambition!' stormed Claire. 'When your father was your age . . . '

'That was thirty years ago,' interrupted Barney. 'The whole structure of society was different then'.

'But what are you going to do?'

'What I want,' shouted Barney, 'is *not* to be asked what I want to do. I do not know. And even if I did, .it would probably be something quite different in a year's time. I just want to find my own way. Maybe Nepal will be as good a place as any other for that. Now, will you please leave me alone?' He took the stairs two at a time. The door of his room slammed behind him. For the next ten minutes, there was a furious twanging on the guitar. Then silence.

★ ★ ★

Katie, her hands occupied in flaking fish for kedgeree, wished that her mind had something else to do than think about Claire. She admitted she had almost certainly been wrong about, first, Margaret and then Veronica. She couldn't afford to be wrong this time. Claire was someone she saw nearly every day, a neighbour, a golfing partner, a woman who had invited her to a party . . . That invitation, reflected Katie, remembrance stiffening her resolution, had not been a gesture of friendship. That invitation had been designed to place her in the right place at the right time. Who had the best opportunity of leaving an envelope on the hall table? Claire herself. Who had left only the envelope, assuming that either Margaret or Katie would know it for what it was? Claire. What more economical method of ensuring that somebody knew she had received a letter without actually revealing the contents? Yes, it had been cleverly set up, the whole thing, and she, Katie, had been the one to fall for it.

She finished the fish and started to shell the hard-boiled eggs. Claire hadn't been noticed at the German post office but Barney could have innocently, incuriously, posted letters for her. She could have found out about Jane Tolworthy from frequent visits to Margaret's house. (Intercepted a phone call? Followed Margaret to Feld-kirchen?) She knew about Veronica's troubles. She, living in the same road, had the best opportunity of seeing Rhodri being followed. And if Joanna had received a letter, who most likely to have sent it? The culminating factor was the motive. There was overwhelming reason to suppose that, driven by pain and frustration, she had set out to destroy marriages happier than her own.

9

In the middle of November, there was an early and unusually heavy snowfall in the Alps. Passes were blocked, roads impassable, villages cut off. But once the snowploughs had got through, the ski resorts sorted themselves out and prepared for that unexpected bonus — an extra few weeks of fleecing the tourists. Which was one reason why Katie was sitting in a corner of a couchette on the Arlberg Express thundering into the night towards the Austrian frontier.

The other reason was that Rhodri had been recalled to London for a ten-day course. 'I won't ask you to come with me,' he said, 'because I'll be busy most of the time and anyway my hours will be unpredictable. You could stay here and play golf every day.' He looked out at the rain-sodden landscape. 'No, maybe not. How about skiing? There ought to be enough snow somewhere.'

There was. Even at Langen, down in the valley, there was snow. Katie stood on the platform in the early morning light and listened to the receding chug of the train making its way into the Arlberg tunnel. Out in the station yard, she handed over suitcase and skis to the driver of the Postbus and dived into the hotel for a mug of steaming chocolate. There were perhaps twenty passengers from the train, standing round the tiled stove, stretching cramped limbs, looking out at the promise of a new day. The driver gave everyone time for a hot drink, then marshalled them into his bus and started the slow crawl up the Flexenstrasse. It was full daylight at Zürs and breakfast-time in Lech. The last stage of the journey was the cable-car to Oberlech and then she was standing in full sunlight, breathing the crisp mountain air, the white slopes falling away below, and all around nothing but peak upon snowy peak. One can't live forever on the heights, she supposed, and maybe one wouldn't want to but — oh, sing hallelujah for that moment of arrival!

Unaware that the long arm of coincidence was beginning to stretch her way, that someone she had once known was at this moment writing Hotel Sonnenschein, Oberlech, Vorarlberg on a luggage label, she shouldered her skis and followed the track which led to the hotel.

★　★　★

Physically tired, glowing with sun and wind and exercise, Katie got back to Oberlech about tea-time. Noticing the suitcases in the foyer, she deduced that there'd been another influx from Langen. If they'd come from England, she thought idly, they had probably flown either to Zürich or Munich and finished the journey by road. There was a couple by the counter, the man signing the register, the woman saying something as she swung around to look out of the long windows at the Kriegerhorn, bathed in the rosy reflection of the setting sun. The same dark hair, brown eyes, enchanting lilt to her voice . . . Katie stopped dead. Where had she heard that description before? Oh no, it couldn't be. Once upon a time there had been Maggy who used to be Meggy (until someone at her new English school pointed out that was only a genteel version of the same name) who presumably had been christened Megan. 'Maggy!' she said disbelievingly.

'Katie! It can't be!'

'What are you doing here?' simultaneously.

'My husband . . . ' began Maggy.

'Rhodri had to do . . . ' said Katie.

'Not Rhodri Rees-Williams?'.

'Why didn't I know it was you?' asked Katie.

'Why should you? He always called me Megan. How extraordinary. Where do we go from here?'

'I have a suggestion.' A slight, sandy-haired man had come up behind Maggy. 'The bar.'

Murdo and Maggy Montgomery had both been married before and both had made a mistake. Realising their good fortune in getting a second chance, they were determined that nothing should go wrong this time. To Katie, seeing them together over the next few days, they seemed to be trying too hard. She hadn't known Maggy particularly well at the Kentish school to which she'd been sent when she was fourteen but they'd been in the same house at Wyndham Abbey. 'You were a prefect when I arrived,' she recalled that first evening. 'I don't think I dared speak to you for the first three months.' She hadn't intended to emphasise the difference in their ages but the look Maggy flashed her was distinctly unfriendly. 'Bogtrotters weren't very popular,' Katie hastened to smooth troubled waters. She remembered how miserable she had been, how much she had missed the rain-washed skies over the lakes and mountains of Killarney and the innate friendliness and self-respect of the people who lived there. She had been homesick for a long time. 'Killarney, I believe, is the Irish Loch Lomond,' said Murdo, coming back with three glasses of glüwein.

Murdo was perhaps forty-five. He had sandy hair of the type that doesn't go grey, and cool pale blue eyes. He was Scots to his finger tips. He was also a first-class skier. 'We have got mountains, you know.' Maggy was a beginner, so Murdo spent the first day seeing her settled in the ski school. The second morning Katie met him by chance at the top of the Kriegerhorn lift.

'Going my way?' he asked and disappeared over the edge. Unthinking, Katie followed. It was only as she shifted her weight forward that she realised she was on a Black Run. Appalled, she focussed on the gradient. The slope, to her eyes, was almost perpendicular. Instinctively she jerked back. Then she fell flat, first of all riding her skis like a toboggan, then turning over and over, gathering speed. One ski came off, then the second as she somersaulted into the safety netting. Winded, she lay and looked at the sky. 'Alright?' asked Murdo. 'I've retrieved your equipment.' On her feet again, she glanced up towards the summit. It still looked incredibly steep.

'There's no way but down,' said Murdo. 'Look — take it in wide turns. Lean right out towards the valley. I'll wait for you at halfway.' Then he'd gone, straight as an arrow. Katie brushed off the snow, clipped on her skis and took a deep breath. The first turn she side-slipped and almost fell, on the second one her parallel skis swung smoothly round. With the third one, she got the rhythm. Leaning so far forward, a slight movement of the shoulders was all that was needed to bring the backs of the skis round. Turns changed to a slight braking. She saw Murdo waiting for her and took the last bit in a straight schuss. Heart pounding, knees shaking, she laughed out loud from sheer relief. He grinned back at her.

'That was worthy of the Cairngorms,' he said.

*   *   *

It was the middle of the week before Katie found herself alone with Maggy. Murdo was taking in a day's helicopter skiing and left immediately after breakfast. There had been a heavy fall of snow overnight and Katie had chosen the wrong time to try off-piste skiing. Ploughing through knee-high snow called for a degree of expertise she'd never yet had to learn. Exhausted and discouraged, she called in at a local bar for beer and a ham roll, and found that Maggy had had the same idea. Katie peeled off her red quilted jacket and white bobble cap and slid onto an upholstered wall-seat. 'You've been falling in soft snow,' said Maggy unsympathetically, 'you should see my bruises!' Katie took a long swig of beer.

'I went through it too,' she said mildly. She looked at Maggy, grey eyes meeting brown. 'We don't have to talk about Rhodri, do we?'

Maggy had been born a Meredith, fourth daughter of a Monmouthshire farmer, as Welsh as her name was Megan. A childless godfather rescued the serious little girl from her happily mud-smeared brothers and sisters and sent her to school in England. Megan repaid his faith and generosity by gaining a scholarship to Oxford, and threw away all academic ambitions when she met Rhodri Rees-Williams on the road to Trelleck.

Maggy finished her drink and lit a cigarette.

'Have you ever been with him to Wales? No? He seems a different person there. If only we could have stayed . . . I didn't transplant very successfully and we just grew apart. I think he

118

needed . . . ' she hesitated momentarily 'a challenge.' No apportioning of blame, just a simple statement of fact.

'You weren't eligible to return to Oxford, were you?' Katie asked. Now that the conversation had taken this turn, she didn't know how to end it.

'Oh no, I'd given up the scholarship. But I got a place at Edinburgh. And that's where I met Murdo. He's a barrister and he came to lecture to our law society.' She smiled, and for a second Katie could imagine that elfin face, short flyaway hair and a voice which had all the music of the valleys bewitching the more earthbound Rhodri of over ten years ago. Then the brooding expression settled back on her face. 'That's the story of my life. Yours hasn't really been written yet, has it?'

Fortunately that cryptic remark required no comment because Maggy's ski instructor came into the bar and she moved over to join him. Katie finished her beer and decided to take the bus over to Zürs and ski back to Lech via the Madlochjoch. Skimming down the long winding piste in the westering sun, she forgot everything but the co-ordination of muscle and mind, the hiss of skis on snow and the flying figures she joined and passed in the final swoop to the village. In the days that followed, a certain pattern evolved. Katie and Murdo tried a route of his choice every morning: each afternoon he took Maggy up one of the easy runs and encouraged her progress. In the evenings Katie joined a party of Americans who had come from Wiesbaden, so she didn't notice that Murdo was becoming increasingly constrained and Maggy rarely laughed. Even if she had, she would never have guessed the reason because it only became apparent on the morning she was due to leave.

Maybe because it was her last run, it was the best one. When she swung to a halt beside Murdo, she pulled off her cap and threw it exultantly in the air.

He looked at the sweep of black hair and the shining eyes and said the words he had never even formed in his own mind. 'I could be very much in love with you.'

'Oh Murdo . . . ' She put her hand on his arm. No good saying how much she liked him, what fun it had been: no point in saying anything at all. She could only think of Rhodri, already on his way back to Germany. Murdo managed a lopsided smile. 'I bet you're thinking,' he said, 'that this sort of thing never happens in the Cairngorms.'

★   ★   ★

There was a happy ending after all. Katie had lunch at the hotel, packed her case and left it at the cable-car station, then prepared to ski down to Lech. She stood at the top of the hill, photographing on her mind the surrounding peaks, memorising the runs, imprinting the line of the straggling village from frozen river to onion-domed church. Each new place retained its special niche in her memory; years afterwards, she could recall a soaring steeple of rock, an alpine chalet, a challenging schuss. She clipped on her skis, poised to run straight to the bus stop at the bottom. As she turned for a last look at Oberlech, a movement caught her eye. Murdo and Maggy had just emerged from the shadow of the cable-car hut, obviously arguing about something. They must have been a hundred yards away but Katie sensed that Maggy was crying. The sound of her voice floated across the snow as she beat with her small fists at her husband's chest. With a small shock of surprise, Katie realised that Maggy at last was acting spon-taneously, uninhibitedly. Maybe a subconscious jealousy had provided the impetus; it didn't matter. Murdo was shouting too, shaking her by the shoulders. Suddenly he turned his head and saw Katie standing at the top of the piste. She waved her ski-stick in salute. He raised his in farewell, then gathered his wife into his arms. Katie projected herself into the first steep, shelving dip and was gone.

10

Sooner or later, it was inevitable that somebody's husband was going to find out about the letters and blow the whole thing sky-high. Fortunately for those who shunned publicity, the explosion occurred in one isolated section of the community and its reverberations were, at first, local.

The weak link was, predictably, Veronica. The cause was potential pregnancy. For nearly six weeks she had hoped. She had got to the stage of thinking in terms of pale blue knitting wool and organdie-trimmed cots. Then she found out that she had miscalculated. It was too much for poor Veronica. When John came home that evening, she threw at him the story of his mistress and son and told him how she knew. John denied it but Veronica was beyond reason. Illogically she threatened to scream the place down if he came near her. If John had slept on it, all would probably have been, if not forgotten, at least postponed for clinical examination. The unmistakable click of the key in the lock of the bedroom door sent him back to the sitting-room and a large whisky. Then he rang up his C.O.

The Colonel had an extension in his bedroom. He also had an inquisitive wife who frequently complained he never told her anything. Happily managing to synchronize lifting of receivers, she sat back and listened. Next morning the news was all round the hospital.

Borne by staff and patients who lived in Niederdorf, it had just begun to penetrate the camp when Katie and Rhodri returned. Rhodri was preoccupied by what he had learnt on the course and how to apply that knowledge to existing circumstances. Katie felt protected by an invisible ray of sun-tanned health and happiness. The ten-day break seemed to have made her immune to doubt and suspicion as well as the usual November viruses. She even wondered how she could have worked so desperately to find the writer. When she heard at the Golf Club that the campaign was no longer a secret, she still refused to worry. After being given an airing, the whole thing would probably blow over. Rhodri never listened to gossip anyway. What she failed to realise was that all was grist to Rhodri's mill. Gossip as gossip didn't interest him but any new item, however small, could contain a particle of information which, when joined by others, could grow into a solid fact. He heard this particular bit of scandal, then forgot about it.

As soon as she returned to number 13 Acacia Avenue, Katie had decided not to tell Rhodri about her meeting with his former wife — anyway, not immediately. It was a spur of the moment decision, taken in the joyful moment of reunion. She just didn't want to spoil the mood. As the days went by, it became increasingly difficult to introduce the subject. She felt that anything she said would be open to misinterpetation. If she enthused about Maggy, could that not lead to comparisons? If she didn't, the inference was that she was being petty-minded. When she talked about her holiday, she did let drop the names Murdo and Maggy Montgomery but there was no reaction from Rhodri other than casual interest, so she left it at that. She would never see them again and they would very soon forget about her. What remained was gratitude to Murdo for his tutelage and his affection, and a conviction that his marriage would endure.

* * *

The state of euphoria cannot last. Katie came down to earth exactly a week after her return. It was soon after breakfast on the first of December and she was drinking a second cup of coffee, gazing out of the dining-room window at the small patch of lawn bounded by the regulation macrocarpa bushes. She didn't hear the sound of footsteps on the path, so the click of the letter-box on the front door made her turn sharply in her chair. It was almost as if someone was there, in the house, with her. All the old fears came sweeping back. Slowly she put down her cup and got to her feet. The envelope was face down on the mat and it was the same size and shape ... Seeing a handwriting she recognised, her relief was so great she didn't immediately take in the significance of the message. 'For obvious reasons,' Margaret Tolworthy had written, 'I prefer not to talk about this on the telephone, but I thought you might like to know that I showed the envelope I received to a friend of ours in Legal Branch who happens to be a calligraphist. He was unwilling to commit himself except in one particular — that the person who addressed the envelope is righthanded.' Well, that didn't mean much, reflected Katie, thinking of Margaret in her sensible rubber-soled shoes taking the trouble to pass on such a generalisation. Halfway up the stairs, she remembered. As clearly as if she was back in the Fordyns' sitting-room, she could see Claire lifting the coffee pot in her left hand. Not only that. Claire was even a left-handed golfer. The inescapable inference was that Claire was not the perpetrator of the poison-pen letters.

*   *   *

So she was right back to the beginning again. As she dressed, Katie realised that her earlier assumption, that the matter would soon be forgotten, was beside the point. The culprit had probably discontinued her activities now that there was a military police guard on the German post office and a roving patrol on the streets, but even that was not the most important thing.

What really mattered was that Joanna had died. And within the next half-hour, there was final proof that she had indeed been one of the known recipients.

It was Claire who came up with the evidence. She called at the house shortly afterwards. 'You were lucky to be away,' she said, pulling off her coat. 'There would have been even more of a riot if the authorities had known about this.' The envelope was addressed to Mrs. Joanna Penshurst at number seventeen Wisteria Walk. It was empty. 'Colin brought it round to me. He said he found it while packing up Joanna's clothes. He'd heard the rumours by then and guessed what it was. He burned the contents unread but couldn't bring himself to destroy the envelope in case there was an official inquiry.' She saw no need to add that Colin did not know about Joanna and Mark. He had simply turned for help to someone he could trust. Katie looked at the address: Mrs. Joanna Penshurst,

603 Niederdorf, Wisteria Walk 17. The same layout as hers, the same printed capitals. But her address hadn't got a 7 in it. 'Claire! Look at that address!' She pointed with a tentative finger at the number of the house. 'Who', she said 'but a continental puts a stroke through a seven!'

★   ★   ★

In a mood of sober triumph they agreed that this was indeed a breakthrough. Not that the writer was necessarily a German because British people who had been abroad a long time were apt to fall into continental habits.

'You mean, like Margaret?' asked Claire, surprised. Katie, who refrained from admitting former suspicions, said hastily that Margaret Tolworthy, like her husband British to the core, would never form other than a solid upright conventional seven, even when writing to her daughter.

'Especially when writing to her

daughter,' she added, 'to emphasise the attitude of no truck with foreigners.'

'So where does that get us?' asked Claire.

'I don't know,' said Katie. In view of the concrete evidence produced by Colin, it was clear that someone was morally guilty of manslaughter.

'I think,' said Claire, revoking her previous decision, 'that we'll have to inform the police, don't you?'

'You'd certainly better hand over Colin's envelope,' Katie agreed. 'That's the vital one.'

'I'll advise him to do that himself,' said Claire, mindful of proper channels. 'As for the rest of us . . . '

'Yes, I know. They'll need all the information they can get. Claire — could you find out the name of the officer in charge of the case? Then I'll go and see him myself. I just want another day to see if I can make anything out of this new clue.'

On the face of it, that continental seven upset all one's preconceived ideas. It was like looking at a painting from a new angle. Change the perspective and you see an entirely different view. She had been trying, by means of elimination, to identify the culprit. She had subsequently looked for a common denominator among the victims. But if you shift the picture a little, how would it look from the angle of motive? The idea that an anti-British German was out to cause disruption was absurd. Besides, where would this hypothetical person have found his or her material? Through Jane Tolworthy's lover? Veronica's *Putzfrau*? Gossip and observation? Katie worked at the problem all morning and resolved to pay another visit to Jane that afternoon.

⋆ ⋆ ⋆

She didn't see Jane after all. By afternoon the situation had radically changed. The letters Katie had received were still in her handbag when, just after lunch, Rhodri accidentally knocked it to the floor. The bundle slithered out like a venomous snake. Rhodri looked at her face. Then he bent down and picked up the top one. She couldn't see which one it was. He read it through. Then he reached for the others, tore them into pieces, threw them into the empty fireplace and put a match to them.

'What bloody nonsense,' he said. 'You don't for a moment think I'd have believed it?'

He looked at the edges beginning to curl, and Katie looked at him. She could see that his brain was getting into gear. Dear God, she prayed, let him stop thinking. Just let him leave it.

'This has been going on for a long time, hasn't it?' he said slowly. She nodded.

'You mean to say you got those letters and never informed the authorities?' His voice was flatly disbelieving. 'A woman committed suicide, didn't she? Was it after getting an anonymous letter?'

Katie nodded again.

'And you just stood by and did nothing?' Rhodri's eyes were the eyes of a stranger. 'I could leave you for that,' he said.

Part Two

1

Katie did the conventional thing. She went home to mother. She would have returned to England anyway because Rhodri told her he had been posted to Washington and had been awaiting confirmation before letting her know about it. In the circumstances, he added, it would be better if he went on ahead and she could join him when he found suitable accommodation. But there was no happy expectation. They came back together and said goodbye at Victoria Station. Rhodri went to a nearby hotel and Katie to Charing Cross to catch a train for Sevenoaks. As the taxi door closed on her isolation, she turned impulsively to make a last minute appeal. But the words wouldn't come. There was no way she could explain without admitting that what the letters had hinted at was true. Rhodri hadn't believed it. He considered her incapable of any shabby action. He trusted her. It was as simple and as heartbreaking as that.

★ ★ ★

Mrs. Delaney had lived in Sevenoaks for all the dozen years which had elapsed since her husband died. Life at Rossmara without him had no attraction for an energetic woman who knew more about running a practice than he did himself. Sean Delaney was an easy-going man and a sympathetic doctor and he didn't deserve to die head-on to the truck of a drunken farmer in the Gap of Dunloe. Katie was already at school in Kent. Mary Delaney sold the house in County Kerry and crossed the Irish Sea for the first time. She was lucky in that it was a buyers' market at the end of the sixties and she was able to acquire, for a reasonable sum, a turn of the century three-storey house in a quiet street leading off the Vine cricket ground. Katie became a day-girl, which suited both mother and daughter, and they let the top floor flat to provide additional income. To keep herself occupied and help with Katie's school bills, Mary converted her large ground-floor drawing-room and opened a nursery school. It had prospered. She now used the dining-room as well and employed an assistant. The flat was used for temporary rather than long-term tenants. It happened to be empty when Katie returned from Germany and she moved straight into it.

An uncomfortably mild January was followed in February by snow and east winds. Katie, uncertain as to her future, helped in the nursery school, spring-cleaned the flat, painted the kitchen and bathroom. She had told her mother about the events of those last three months at Niederdorf and never referred to them again. The affair of the poison pen had ceased to matter. She heard infrequently from Rhodri, short and factual letters which told her nothing. She knew she was drifting and there was nothing she could do about it.

★ ★ ★

What finally woke her up was a letter from Claire. It came via their London bank which Rhodri had left as a forwarding address. The grape-vine had obviously been active because Claire knew she had not accompanied Rhodri to Washington. After various items of local news, she went on to say that the poison pen had not yet been found. 'As far as I know,' Claire wrote, 'there has not been another outbreak, so presumably it was Joanna's suicide which scared the writer off. However, it's an unpleasant feeling that someone you know, possibly even meet every day, was the one responsible for sending Joanna to her death.' She didn't mention Mark or Barney but ended by saying that Margaret Tolworthy's sister-in-law lived near Sevenoaks and, if Katie should come across her, it would be better not to mention the affair of the letters. Katie's first reaction was a faint stirring of interest. It was in a way a confirmation of her own theory that the case would only be solved by someone familiar with the background of the people involved. The police had the facilities for investigation and surveillance but how would they tackle the questions of opportunity and motive? Besides, the trail was already cold by the time they had been called in. Thoughtfully, Katie went down to do her morning stint with the three-to four-year-olds.

'Do you know anyone in the district called Tolworthy?' she asked her mother when they were snatching a brief respite.

'There's a Miss Tolworthy up at Ide Hill. I met her once at a charity function. Unpleasant-looking female. Yes, someone said she has a brother serving in Germany. They're an old

Army family and she's the most militant of them all. Would you like me to ask her over for coffee?'

'Heaven forbid,' said Katie. 'She might frighten the children.'

For the next few days the wintry weather continued. Then one morning Katie looked out of her kitchen window, across the rooftops to the countryside beyond and saw the weald above the distant Pilgrim's Way hazed with pearly sunshine. It was a day to share. She felt the familiar aching sense of loss. If only once Rhodri would say he missed her . . . Angrily she blinked the tears from her eyes. What she needed was exercise — to walk and walk till she was too tired to care. She locked the front door of the flat, went down the outside staircase, waved at the children through the drawing-room window and backed the car out through the laurels. Then she took the road which led to Ide Hill.

★   ★   ★

The encounter with Brigadier Tolworthy's sister was pure coincidence, and it left a nasty taste. Unpleasant was the word Mary Delaney had used. The one that occurred to Katie was malicious.

Someone mentioned the name Tolworthy as she sat drinking beer and eating a sandwich in a pub at the top of Ide Hill. Because of Claire's letter, Katie looked idly over her shoulder. Two women were sitting at a table in a corner near the bar. One was blonde and plump and obviously not happy. The other had tinted auburn hair, close-set eyes and a discontented mouth. Katie couldn't hear what she was saying, but from the expression on her face she wasn't enjoying her drink. Katie turned back to her beer and a view of the car park. She would probably have left it at that if the blonde woman hadn't happened to pass her table on her way to the Ladies. Even then, under normal circumstances, she would have ignored the woman in the corner. But she'd had an unrewarding tramp up and down hill, her mood had made a mockery of the near-spring sunshine and the sandwich had turned to cardboard in her mouth. Prospects for the afternoon were equally arid. Any scrap of information she required could be a straw in the wind if she still wanted to solve the case which had brought her to the present impasse. So she picked up her tankard and strolled over to the bar. When she reached the table, she hesitated. 'Miss Tolworthy? Miss Eleanor Tolworthy?' The older woman looked at her suspiciously. 'I heard the name . . . You must be Brigadier Tolworthy's sister.'

'You've met my brother?'

'Yes. But I know his wife rather better. We've played golf together.'

'Margaret,' snapped Miss Tolworthy, 'was quite the wrong wife for him. The family never approved of her. It's all a matter of tradition, of course.' Katie realised she was still hovering on one foot with an empty tankard in her hand. 'Well, it's been nice . . . I'll tell them

I've seen you when I go back to Germany.' And that, reflected Katie, was three palpable untruths in the space of sixteen words. The result, however, was exactly as she had expected. That last word was a powerful lure. Eleanor Tolworthy was probably kept short of news from the German end.

'You must have a drink with me. George!' She snapped her fingers, 'two gin and tonics'.

The blonde woman didn't return. She probably knew the back way out of the Ladies. George didn't look too pleased at being summoned from behind his bar but he got his own back by serving doubles.

'What part of Germany?' asked Eleanor. Her eyes were watchful.

'Niederdorf,' said Katie and waited.

'Is your husband an Army man?' Obviously she was asking for credentials, Katie reckoned, before blasting off about Margaret. She was tempted to make Rhodri an Admiral — maybe an

Air Commodore? No, life was complicated enough.

'He's a civilian,' she answered. Interest immediately evaporated. One could see Miss Tolworthy was beginning to regret the expense of a gin.

'Then he wouldn't know my brother,' she said indifferently. Katie could have pointed out that civilians too know other people but she didn't.

'No. My husband's interests are rather more esoteric,' she said smoothly. Two could play at being bitchy. She began to wish she'd never invited this exchange.

'Is Margaret bearing up? Doubtless you know her family history. I'm surprised the instability hasn't been passed on to the daughter. Has Jane found a suitable partner?' She made it sound like a set of Lancers, thought Katie. Which was very likely how she saw the mating game. Katie considered Jane, cohabitating blissfully with her German mechanic.

'Very suitable,' she said steadily. She

finished her drink and got to her feet.

'And what is your name?' asked Miss Tolworthy. Katie made a business of collecting her bag but she was thinking that it would serve no purpose for either Margaret or Jane to hear of her intervention.

'Ponsonby-Fitzwilliam,' she answered clearly. 'The Gloucestershire branch.'

Suddenly, standing in the car park, she was blazingly angry. She didn't doubt Eleanor Tolworthy's story — it could easily be checked. Eleanor had intimated that there was insanity in Margaret's family. She had enjoyed passing on that information to a stranger. She had obviously not considered Margaret good enough for Henry. It would give her intense pleasure to learn of the poison-pen campaign, the nasty old bat. Katie shook her fist at the bland and milky sky. Like Maggy, who had lost her inhibitions in a jealous rage, she felt free to be herself. She was alive again and ready for action. Without looking back, she drove away.

It was with a sense of inevitability that she recognised the car standing at the kerb outside the house in Vine Court Road. She had been a passenger in that one several times. It belonged to the Hon. Patrick Darran.

*　★　*

Mary Delaney heard the doorbell ring just after halfpast twelve. The younger children, who only came in the morning, had already been collected by their mothers, the others were drinking milk and eating each other's sandwiches. The tall stranger on the doorstep instantly dissolved into the tow-headed little boy from the big house by the river just beyond Rossmara. 'Patrick!' she exclaimed with much pleasure. 'How you've grown!'

'It happens to the best of us.' He smiled at her. 'You're looking very well, Mrs. Delaney. I hear you've got Katie staying with you?'

'Yes, she's living in the top flat. Come

on in. Have you driven up from Dover? Katie's out at the moment but you must stay and have lunch with me.' She led the way to a small, comfortably-furnished room overlooking the garden at the rear. 'I'll get you a drink. I've even got some Guinness ... ' Left alone, Patrick wandered over to the window. It was a garden geared to the needs of children, he could see, with a swing, a sandpit, an ancient acacia to climb. Acacia Avenue ... He still wasn't sure if he had done the right thing in coming here.

He didn't know how he had expected Katie to look. He had been on attachment in Berlin when she and Rhodri left Germany for, it was reported, America. Subsequent rumours, that Rhodri had departed for Washington alone, had gone the rounds. Then he had met Claire Fordyn at a party and she told him she'd heard Katie was with her mother. He had long since known that Mrs. Delaney was in Sevenoaks. Finding the address was a mere formality. When Katie came in soon after lunch, he knew that this was not the time to tell her. 'Kent seems to suit you too,' he said lightly.

'Patrick!' She held out her hands. 'Lovely to see you. I gather mother's taken care of you. Come and have coffee in my flat. I want you to see it.'

He didn't speak of Rhodri till they were drinking coffee on the wide window-seat in the lofty living-room. From where he was sitting, he could see a bell-tower on a building down the street, a red-tiled roof and a cypress tree. With the blue hills beyond, it was like an aquatint of Tuscany. He wondered if Katie had been to Florence or seen the horses race round the sun-baked streets of Siena . . . He put down his coffee cup.

'What happened?' he asked abruptly. Katie didn't prevaricate.

'He found out,' she answered.

'Before you reported it,' deduced Patrick.

'The worst thing to bear,' she said,

turning her head away, 'was that he didn't believe what the letters insinuated. I had no defence. I couldn't even explain my reasons for the actions I took to try and clear up the whole mess before anyone else got hurt. Oh I know now that I was wrong.' She got up and walked over to the other dormer window. 'In his eyes, I wasn't merely irresponsible, I was lacking in common humanity.' She swung around and her grey pleated skirt swirled with her. 'I nearly sank under the burden of conscience. But not any more. Whatever I did, I've paid for it. I still intend to solve that case, and when I have the answer I'll take it across the Atlantic.'

'I see the way your mind is working,' agreed Patrick. 'There's nothing like a successful conclusion for justifying one's methods.' Unhurriedly he got to his feet. He looked at the red and blue reindeer rollicking across her silver-grey sweater. He looked into her wide grey eyes. 'Darling Katie, don't ever change.' He was standing close to her now. For the first time she was aware that they were alone. A car went by on the road outside. A child called out. She could hear the tick of the carriage clock on the mantelpiece. Patrick kissed her gently on the mouth. She put up a hand and touched his face.

'I'll ring the bell', he said, 'when I get back from Rossmara'.

But he didn't ring. He didn't even write. She wondered later if that had been his way of saying goodbye. Because ten days afterwards his engagement was announced in the Irish Times.

2

As soon as Patrick had gone, Katie put her resolve into action. She sat down at the table in the bay window with three sheets of foolscap. On one she wrote down what she knew about the case, on the second her deductions. The third she kept for evidence against yet another name. She spent a long time thinking about the continental seven which had figured in Joanna's address and decided not to use it as a starting point, chiefly because it opened up too many avenues she was unable to follow. She was convinced that, when she finally got the answer, that seven would drop into its preordained slot. In the end, she was quite right about that.

She was thinking about Margaret Tolworthy next morning when the postman arrived. Even if there had been a history of insanity, it need not

155

necessarily be hereditary. On the other hand, it had to be taken into account. If the culprit were Margaret, there would probably be another outbreak sometime, somewhere. One could only keep in touch and hope that Henry's retirement would bring a more relaxed way of life. But it was the present that mattered — and a result. There was literally no way, other than a confession, of proving that Margaret had been involved. Her thoughts lingered. It didn't actually have to be a confession. If she could only face Margaret once more and ask her a question, she would know. Probably through something quite small, as Patrick had once suggested — a tone of voice, a flicker of expression, a betraying movement of the hands. Suddenly it seemed imperative that she should see Margaret again.

The morning mail brought an unexpected bonus. It came in the form of an invitation card in which Miss Tolworthy requested the pleasure of the company of Mrs. Delaney and Mrs. Rees-Williams for cocktails on Wednesday March the fourth at 6.30 p.m. On the back was written 'By request of Henry and Margaret who will be staying with me.'

'The only snag,' said Katie, showing it to her mother, 'is that Miss Tolworthy will immediately recognise me as as Mrs. Ponsonby-Fitzwilliam. The Gloucestershire branch,' she added. Mary Delaney's eyes sparkled.

'Could he have been your first husband?' she suggested. 'Killed in a hunting accident? No — a much better idea. What were you wearing then? Skirt and sweater? And your hair on your shoulders? And no make-up? Well, she's not going to recognise you at all if you do the thing properly. Or at least she won't be sure and you only have to act as though you'd never met before. Now, first of all the hairdresser, you'd better make an appointment.'

Katie's hair was swept into a smooth pleat, held on top of her head by a jewelled comb. Silver shadowed her eyes and accentuated her cheekbones. Brigadier Tolworthy greeted her with unfeigned pleasure; his sister's lips quivered on the edge of recognition. Margaret looked pleased to see her too. Then they were mingling with the other guests. She would have to choose her moment, Katie realised, if she wanted to talk to Margaret in private. For the first hour she circulated, introduced by her mother who was instantly at home with the parents and grandparents of all her children. Henry Tolworthy brought her another drink and asked her when she was planning to join Rhodri. Eleanor Tolworthy ignored her. Finally, Margaret detached her from a posse of retired generals and manoeuvred her into an open space. They talked about Niederdorf and the Golf Club and the Fordyns. Henry replenished their glasses. A deprecating relative ('Cousin Agnes, poor thing,' said Margaret) offered ample if unimaginative savouries ('I wasn't allowed to help,' said

Margaret). People passed and repassed like water swirling round an island. Katie could see Eleanor, indefatigable hostess, working her way down the room, all set to separate those who were enjoying themselves. There wasn't much time.

'There haven't been any more letters?' she asked. Margaret shook her head.

'No. I, like Claire, think that Joanna's death really frightened the writer. Incidentally, you were quite right when you advocated informing the authorities. One didn't at the time — I can see that now — like being advised by someone both younger and a comparative newcomer.'

'And I had no right . . . ' began Katie.

'You were right to suspect anyone and everyone. I even thought you had your eye on Claire. That's why I let you know the calligraphist's findings.' Her smile was warm and understanding and Katie was suddenly, completely, satisfied. Why should Margaret go out of her way to exonerate Claire when she herself was right-handed? Double bluff? No, Margaret hadn't that sort of mind. Rhodri, yes, and she herself too because she knew something of his world, but Tolworthy reasoning was straightforward.

'One more thing,' said Margaret, 'before my sister-in-law drags you off to meet someone you don't want to know ... You will doubtless be informed of instability in my family. The eccentric was my paternal grandfather who decamped to Monte Carlo with the gamekeeper's daughter.'

Driving home, mother and daughter spent a companionable few minutes enumerating Eleanor's less lovable qualities. Back at Vine Court Road, they changed into housecoats and settled down in the warm kitchen to soup and cheese and gossip. Mary Delaney, still at fifty without a grey hair, reported one dishonourable proposal and three luncheon invitations.

'Retired generals are apt to be mildly naughty, aren't they? In a rather endearing sort of way. I liked the look of Margaret Tolworthy.'

'Yes, she was quite matey. Odd how people change when you meet them out of context, if you know what I mean. Incidentally, I'm finally convinced that she had nothing — apart from being a recipient — to do with the poison-pen letters. Which leaves me precisely where I started.' Her mother got up to make coffee. Katie collected the plates and took them over to the sink. Mary Delaney had been lucky in that the kitchen had been completely renovated shortly before she bought the house. The Aga had been retained but surrounded by white painted units which gleamed against the red tiles of the floor. The chairs too had been painted red and the table was white. It was the true living-room now that the two larger ground-floor rooms had been commandeered. Katie was still preoccupied.

'Looking at it all from a distance,' she reflected, 'the whole set-up was really a bit childish — cutting words out of newspapers, popping envelopes through letter boxes, rather like ringing door-bells and running away.' She stiffened. A couple of knives clattered to the floor. 'I wonder.' It was that phrase of Claire's which pointed the way. 'Someone you know, possibly even meet every day'. Who did Claire see every day? 'It could have been Barney,' she breathed.

★ ★ ★

Mary Delaney measured coffee into the percolator.

'He's sixteen, isn't he? Does he get on with his parents?'

'I think so,' Katie said doubtfully. 'His father's apt to shout at him, but as far as I could see he took absolutely no notice. He just went his own way.'

'Now that parental opposition is, in most cases, non-existent, there's nothing to rebel against, is there?'

'I wonder', speculated Katie, 'if he secretly resented not going to public school? Could he have an adolescent grudge against society?' She sat down again at the table. Her newly swept-up hair began to escape in wisps round her ears. 'What could be easier than leaving the letter to his mother on the hall table? Especially on the evening of the party with a whole roomful of suspects. He could have observed me going out before planting one through my letter-box. He was even reported by his chum Gary as being seen at the *Postamt*.' Her mother brought over two cups of coffee.

'There's another thing,' said Katie suddenly. 'He speaks German. He has German friends. He probably uses the continental seven without thinking about it.' She went on, speaking her thoughts aloud. 'He could have found out about Jane from Germans he knew. He'd know about Veronica's problems from Golf Club gossip. He could have followed me. He probably guessed about Mark and Joanna — he must have known there was something wrong with his parents' marriage.' She clasped her hands round her coffee cup. 'But I like Barney,' she said unhappily. 'And what would happen to Claire if she lost her son as well as her husband?'

*　　*　　*

Claire Fordyn would quite happily have lost her son that evening. Having said he was going to be out, he had turned up in the middle of a dinner party. And not only turned up but barged into the dining-room, having obviously forgotten there was anything on. One resigned, one furious and four polite faces turned in his direction as he stood there in his dirtiest jeans with his mouth open and his thatch of hair falling over his eyes. Mark, fortunately, was speechless with anger. The guests, likewise parents of sons, sat there smugly thinking of their own bright and well-mannered offspring safely at prep or in dormitory on the other side of the nice wide English channel. Claire did her best. 'Was it advanced German tonight?' she said brightly and gave him no time to answer. 'Get yourself something to eat in the kitchen. Now, please Barney,' with a touch of steel in the voice. Barney got himself out of the room without falling over his feet. Mark poured out more wine. Everyone started talking. The episode was forgotten.

But not by Claire. If only Barney could just for once have looked presentable and behaved in a civilised manner. It wasn't altogether his fault, she had to admit. In recent months he had been set up as a sort of buffer state between husband and wife — and you haven't time to acquire poise when you live between two warring states. The fact that it was a war of attrition merely added to the tension. Sometimes she felt that she'd be thankful when Barney finally did leave home. While he was still there to be cajoled, fed, shouted at, occasionally treasured, he was the symbol of normal family life. When he had gone, she and Mark would come face to face in a silent house. That was when they would have to work out a way of living together — or settle for a divorce.

★   ★   ★

Mark was not insensitive to atmosphere but it was easier for a man who was out of the house most days and could, if necessary, find plausible reasons for absence after working hours, to maintain the fiction that theirs was a reasonable marriage. Or, at any rate, no better or worse than many in the same street. He sometimes felt that if only Claire wouldn't be so nice and tolerant and determinedly bright, he might be able to get through to her. He had betrayed and hurt her, yes — but he couldn't go on being in the wrong for ever. In fact, he knew just how lucky he had been in coming through comparatively unscathed. It would have done his career no good at all if the truth had come out; he might even have been asked to resign his commission. And despite the feeling of being trapped in an entirely predictable profession, it was the only job he knew and he didn't want to lose it. He hadn't got flair like, for example, Patrick Darran, but he was an able administrator and he got on well with the men. He'd known just how much he wanted to stay in the Army when he'd read the anonymous letter sent to Joanna and seen that he had been mentioned by name.

Joanna had been special. He could never deny that. And now he would always remember her as a single perfect episode in his life. But he was realist enough to know it could never have lasted. Descent from the heights must eventually have followed, either through Joanna's conscience or the ever-present fear of discovery. What he needed now was what he had always had with Claire — daily companion-ship and love and laughter. He couldn't remember the last time they had laughed together . . .

★ ★ ★

Barney was not insensitive either. He knew perfectly well the impression he had made at the dinner party. He also realised that in the last few months ninety percent of conversation in the home had been his parents talking to each other through him. He sometimes wondered what would happen when he left.

Barney considered that a formal education would put him at a disadvantage with the members of the rock group he intended to join as soon as he got away from Niederdorf, but he had resigned himself to finishing the school year. Talk of Nepal was only a smokescreen he put up for the benefit of his father and mother. Anything far enough away, preferably with a tang of masculine adventure, would keep them happy while he made plans for what he really wanted to do. They thought that any adolescent could twang a guitar: they had no idea how good he really was, just as they didn't know what he did with most of his free time. They were so busy not speaking to each other that he reckoned he could get away with murder. If it wasn't for Lindy, life would be fairly crummy and even she was only stringing him along to get away from her father. Most of his contemporaries, he reflected, seemed to have problem parents. Even Gary had taken the job at the BP place because his mother considered it demeaning — whatever that meant. If Gary had any sense he'd take his earnings and really see what it was like in Nepal or Mogadishu or Nevada before incarcerating himself at some grimy redbrick university. Not the life for Barney Fordyn, no future in it. For a rock star, there was a whole listening world.

Hearing signs of movement from the dining-room, he hacked a slice of beef off the joint, stuffed it between two pieces of bread and loped up the stairs. At least he could do as he liked in his own room.

He was still awake when the guests, in happy mood, departed around midnight. There were the usual sounds of clearing up — glasses clinking, ashtrays emptied into the dustbin, chain on the front door — and as his parents came upstairs he caught a few remarks of the pass-the-mustard variety. Then silence. They didn't even quarrel about him. Somehow that was more disquieting than if they had. Before he went to sleep, he thought of his mother's desperate attempt at face-saving. The funny thing was that the German group in Feldkirchen he practised with really did have advanced technique.

3

If Rhodri's father hadn't died when he did, things might have turned out very differently. It was a heart attack at the end of a long day's work. He was found by his secretary slumped over his desk in the consulting rooms near the centre of Birmingham. The shock was all the greater in that he was an active man with no history of heart trouble. His widow sent an immediate cable to Rhodri but did not know her daughter-in-law's present address. Rhodri arrived back from America on the morning of the funeral.

Neither Katie nor her mother read the obituaries in their daily newspaper. Katie had met her in-laws maybe half-a-dozen times but had never got to know them. Mr. Rees-Williams was a busy man, and his wife had not welcomed an Irish wife for her son any more than the Welsh one who had preceded her. Determinedly English, the only impetuous action of her life had been marriage to a Welshman and she had never forgiven herself for it. On the day of the funeral, Katie played her first game of golf since leaving Germany. When she returned, her mother told her that the telephone in the flat had rung a couple of times. 'If it's important,' she added, 'doubtless whoever it was will ring again.'

'It might be Patrick,' said Katie, unzipping her anorak. 'He expected to be back in about a week. D'you know, I might never have held a club in my hand, I played so badly today. But it's a lovely course for all that it's called Wildernesse. Are there muffins for tea?' She ran a comb through her hair and noticed the colour in her face and the brightness of her eyes.

'There's the doorbell. Have Emily and Luke been collected yet? Come on, you two!' So that was how Rhodri saw her, standing in the doorway, laughing in the sunlight, holding a small hand in each of hers. For once in his life he, the articulate, the cosmopolitan, found that he had nothing to say.

★   ★   ★

Rhodri's grief went deeper than he would have believed possible. Father and son had always been close, ever since the days of their joyful escape to the farmhouse near Trelleck. Though they hadn't seen each other for more than brief visits in recent years, the bond was something which endured. The news of his death was more than a shock, it seemed to him like the end of an era. He didn't ask Katie to attend the funeral simply because it never entered his mind. But once he was alone with his mother in the large detached house on the edge of what had once been countryside, he suddenly ached for someone to share his loss. He realised that his mother's sorrow was chiefly for her changed circumstances and already she was planning to sell the house and buy herself a bungalow somewhere on the south coast. Rhodri stayed long enough to give her what practical help she needed. Then he set out for Sevenoaks.

⋆ ⋆ ⋆

He was wearing a black tie. As soon as she saw that, Katie knew what had happened. All animation seemed to have drained from his face. She, who had never been to Wales, was eerily reminded of the corporate face of the pithead crowd after a mine disaster. The children, sensing something beyond their comprehension, scampered back into the hall. Katie moved into his arms. 'Oh darling,' she said, 'I'm so sorry.'

Mary Delaney had kept in touch with the few relations and many friends she had left behind in Ireland. Over the years some had moved away, a couple had died and one or two had stopped corresponding. But any news of outstanding interest found its way to Vine Court Road as fast as first class mail could take it. On the evening of Rhodri's arrival, the three of them had supper in the big kitchen on the ground floor. The table was covered with a red-and-white checked cloth, and they drank a bottle of wine with Mary's special *quiche*. Rhodri looked more relaxed, his face had lost its strain. Katie, to her mother's eyes, was the one who hadn't yet had time to make adjustments.

'I haven't had time to tell you yet,' said Mary, passing round the salad, 'I had a couple of letters from Rossmara by the second post. Patrick has just got engaged to Grania Drumcarrig! His father must be very pleased. He always wanted Patrick to marry.' Katie's hand reached out towards her glass. She suddenly looked as if some inner conflict had been resolved. 'I haven't seen her since I was about eight,' she said composedly.

'I happened to see her in Bond Street a year or so ago.' Mary Delaney sipped her wine. 'She was a plain little girl, wasn't she? Well, she's a plain young woman but it's an arresting face. It's got character and distinction.' Grania, she thought, had an elegant sufficiency which would be matched by Patrick's easy authority.

'Doesn't she work on the Morning Post?' Rhodri asked unexpectedly. 'In fact, she once wrote an article on rugby — from the point of view of the wives. Though, to be honest, she seemed to know quite a bit about the game itself.' The surprise in his voice brought a smile to Katie's face. Rhodri was recovering. And soon they would go up to the flat and life would be normal again and there would be a definite future.

Later that evening Katie stood by the bay window in the living-room. She was wearing her yellow housecoat and her hair was tied back with a tawny ribbon. She knelt on the window-seat and looked out at the night. By the light of the street-lamp, raindrops twinkled in the puddles and glittered like diamonds on the bare branches. She thought about Rhodri and herself, not necessarily agreeing or always approving but tied together by vows not easily broken.

'Katie?' She turned her head. Rhodri was standing in the doorway. He was wearing a towelling dressing-gown she hadn't seen before. But the line of head and shoulder, the way his hair grew back off his forehead, the strength of his arms, all these were deeply familiar.

'You look different,' he said. They looked at each other. 'Vive *la différence*!'

★ ★ ★

The next twenty-four hours were quietly happy. Rhodri relaxed for the first time since he had heard of his father's death. He and Katie drove to Toy's Hill and walked through the bluebell woods which were just beginning to show a tantalizing promise of next month's sapphire carpet. They talked tentatively of the future. Katie would apply for a visa, Rhodri would lease a flat or small house. That evening he took Katie and her mother out to dinner at a pub in the High Street which was crowded and cheerful and full of life and laughter. Katie was humming a tune as she ran up the outside staircase and into the flat ahead of Rhodri. The telephone rang as she reached the sitting-room door and, without bothering to turn on the light, she moved swiftly forward and took up the receiver. 'Hullo?' she said. And again, quickly, 'Hullo?' Nobody spoke. But it wasn't a dead silence. Just like it happened in Germany, she thought in sudden horror. There was somebody at the other end, listening, breathing. She heard footsteps on the wooden stairs. Rhodri mustn't see her like this. Even in the dark, he would sense that something was wrong. She ran for the bathroom, closed the door behind her and locked it. She turned on the taps and sat down on the edge of the bath. Things that had been pushed to the back of her mind emerged, came out into the open. Whom had Rhodri met that night in the forest last summer? Who had telephoned him just before he left? Had a word been spoken or was the ringing merely a signal? Only one person could answer those questions. Rhodri himself.

She thought she heard someone call out but pretended not to have heard. Yet she couldn't just stay there. Slowly she got to her feet, brushed back her hair, put on more lipstick, finally turned off the taps. The light was on in the living-room, spilling out into the corridor. She turned into the kitchen. 'How about a nightcap?' she called and was thankful that her voice appeared normal. What was she going to do, she asked herself urgently. Could she just forget that episode in their lives? Never find out the truth? And, by the same token, let him go on thinking she knew nothing about it? Even more important and only now acknowledged, was the fact that they had not yet spoken of the cause of their estrangement. Forgiveness had been implicit in their reconciliation the previous night but she hadn't told Rhodri about the result of her investigations — or even that she had done anything about the matter from the very beginning. There are things, she thought, we can't talk about, will never be able to talk about. Does it matter so much? Shouldn't there be an element of privacy in every relationship? Was putting it into words worth risking her marriage? Because Rhodri wouldn't come back a second time.

'Whisky and soda for me', he said, appearing in the doorway behind her. She took the bottle of whisky out of the corner cupboard. 'Help yourself, darling', she said. 'I'm just going to have a bath.' It could be that she was buying time. But she knew that she had already made up her mind.

Next morning she drove him to the station. He was planning to call in at headquarters in London and fly out that evening. The train was already signalled when she drew the car to a halt. There was only time for a hurried goodbye at the window of the compartment. She stood on the draughty platform till the train was out of sight.

She left the car outside the house and walked up the High Street. The first thing she did was to obtain from a travel agent an application form for an American visa. Then she had her hair cut and shaped round her head and across her forehead. Finally she treated herself to a martini at the Chequers bar. She drank to the future.

4

Exactly three weeks after her party, Eleanor Tolworthy was murdered. Her body was found the following morning by her thrice-weekly cleaning woman who had a key to the back door. She had been strangled by the chiffon scarf she happened to be wearing round her neck. Mrs. Palfrey, arriving punctually at eight-thirty, had been alerted by the chaos in the drawing-room of 'Little Sandhurst' but the discovery still came as a nasty shock. Not, however, incapacitating. After telephoning the police, she was able to bounce back sufficiently to pass on the news to cronies in neighbouring houses. One such house belonged to a couple whose little girl attended the kindergarten in Vine Court Road. Which was how Katie and her mother were among the first to be informed. Being mere acquaintances of the dead woman, they were not immediately involved and learned little more than what was reported in Friday's national press. The real sensation was postponed till Saturday.

The Sevenoaks Post was a weekly paper, inadequately staffed but not lacking initiative. The assistant editor and general dogsbody enthusiastically took on the job of crime reporter and his was the headline which screamed across the front page on Saturday morning. 'Who is Mrs. Ponsonby-Fitzwilliam?'

* * *

The Post came out every Saturday. From the staff's point of view, the murder could not have been more conveniently timed. If it had happened earlier, interest would have waned by the weekend whereas Thursday or, worse still, Friday would not have left sufficient working hours for the collection, interpretation and presentation of the more sensational items. Presentation, the crime reporter felt, was all. The facts had been reported elsewhere on Thursday and Friday, so a new approach was definitely needed. There was no obvious suspect, nor was there a clear motive. The burglar theory never got off the ground as there was no trace of unlawful entry. Miss Tolworthy must have admitted the killer herself. Whether the disorder surrounding the body was meant to confuse the issue or whether a desperate search really had been made, the police were not yet prepared to say. Miss Tolworthy's only relatives were a brother and his family who were in Germany at the relevant time, and she appeared to have no close friends. The story had looked to be dying of sheer lack of material when the crime reporter managed to obtain interviews with the next-door neighbours of the deceased. As 'Little Sandhurst' stood in three acres of orchard and woodland, and those adjoining were similarly blessed, the houses were at least a couple of hundred yards apart and none of the occupants had seen or heard anything out of the ordinary — or, indeed, anything at all — on the Wednesday night. But one of them had been persuaded to talk.

★ ★ ★

Katie, appalled, stared at the front page of the newspaper her mother had tossed, unread, on the kitchen table. Her eyes dropped down the page. 'Fair-haired, Junoesque, 46, Mrs. Vivienne Ridley, a widow, told me that she sometimes had a drink with Miss Tolworthy at the Sennock Arms at the top of the hill. They were having a friendly chat one day about a month ago . . . ' So *that* was it. Plump, artificially blonde and well over fifty, the unhappy-looking woman who had been sitting with Eleanor Tolworthy and who had later gone away. Gone out, amended Katie, but obviously not away. Mrs. Ridley must have hovered just inside the door leading to the Ladies, not wanting to interrupt but obviously determined to outstay the interloper. Presumably she had nipped into the loo before Katie herself emerged on her way to the car park. 'Mrs. Ridley,' the report continued, 'said she went out to powder her nose and, as she was coming back, she saw another woman at the table and heard voices raised in anger and then the woman tell Miss Tolworthy that her name was Ponsonby-Fitzwilliam, the Gloucestershire branch. Mrs Ridley saw her only briefly but described her as youngish with long black hair, wearing a grey skirt and red anorak. There is no record of anyone of that name and description in the home counties, let alone Gloucestershire. Who,' demanded the indefatigable reporter, 'is the mystery woman and what was the subject of her quarrel with the deceased?'

Horrified, incredulous, Katie dropped the paper. This just couldn't be happening! She hadn't been quarrelling with Eleanor. The tone at times had been slightly acrimonious but not so that anyone would notice. Anyone? Where had the barman been? What about the other people in the room? She couldn't recall their faces but there had been quite a few of them. One thing she was thankful for — she hadn't taken off her anorak. The grey sweater with the red and blue reindeer would have stood out like a beacon. Thankfulness was short-lived. What she had read was bad enough. There was worse to come.

★ ★ ★

She steeled herself to keep on reading. As soon as she picked up the paper again, her eye was caught by the heading above the penultimate paragraph. There were two words: 'Esoteric tastes.' According to the newsprint, Mrs. Ridley stated that the mystery woman was referring to her husband.

What did the damage was her next sentence. 'It doesn't sound quite nice, somehow.' If she hadn't been so shocked, Katie could have admired the skill with which the case against Mrs. Ponsonby-Fitzwilliam was being built up. She had threatened Miss Tolworthy, she was probably using a false name, she had since disappeared. What was more, she had a husband with unmentionable habits . . . She could imagine the speculations. Could Miss Tolworthy have interrupted an orgy? Maybe the unsavoury pair had killed her for a possible hoard hidden in her drawing-room. Or, more likely, compromising photographs. The whole thing was so monstrous that Katie was torn between incredulous laughter and screaming hysterics. What she did was to pour herself an outsize tot of medicinal brandy. That at least put paid to the hysterics. She moved through to the hallway and caught sight of her reflection in the oval mirror opposite the front door. An unfamiliar face stared back at her. She still hadn't got used to the difference a simple haircut could make. Swept low across her forehead, it subtly emphasised the contours and made her eyes look enormous. It suddenly struck her that Mrs. Ridley would be most unlikely to recognise the Mrs. Ponsonby-Fitzwilliam she had glimpsed on one occasion and then for not more than a few moments.

Within the next quarter of an hour, this impression had been confirmed. Walking down Hollybush Lane towards the local bakery, she met an acquaintance who looked at her with a puzzled frown and passed without speaking. She bought fresh rolls for lunch and a bag of apples at the shop on the corner and walked thoughtfully back up the road. The sun sailed out from behind a gilt-edged cloud and fused an overspill of forsythia into a brilliant explosion of yellow. She lifted her face gratefully to the warmth and the colour. Maybe she had been panicking unnecessarily. The next edition of the Post was a whole week away and the case might have been solved by then: and the name Ponsonby-Fitzwilliam relegated to a basement archive. There was no need — no need at all — to become involved.

Mary Delaney had other ideas about that. She had read the article while Katie was out and absorbed the initial impact. As they sat eating egg mayonnaise with rolls and cheese at the white-painted kitchen table, she gave her opinion.

'A journalistic stunt, of course', she said, 'and an effective one, especially in a community small enough for most people to know each other by sight. I suppose you did use the word esoteric?'

'I did.' Katie buttered the bread for which she had little appetite. 'But not even using it in its proper sense. All I was trying to infer was that Rhodri — whom thank heaven I didn't mention by name — had more interesting things to do than scraping acquaintance with Brigadier Tolworthy.

Nice man he may be and a good officer but intellectually limited. It's a pity,' she added bitterly, 'that I didn't put it in just those words. Eleanor would have been furious but at least Mrs. Ridley would have understood what I was talking about. Presumably she equates the word with erotic — and she's not going to be the only one!'

'What,' asked her mother gently, 'are you going to do?' Katie put down her fork. 'I don't see,' she said, 'how it would serve the cause of justice for me to identify myself. I had nothing, even indirectly, to do with the crime.' Mary Delaney waited till she had chosen and peeled a banana. 'There is one thing that occurs to me,' she said at last. 'This red herring may take up unnecessary public time — time which should be spent in tracking down the murderer. Another thing; there would be much less unpleasantness if you went to them voluntarily than if you were eventually identified. Oh, I know how different you look with your hair short, but your voice hasn't changed nor your way of moving. Do you want to be forever looking over your shoulder? I know how you fear the publicity, my dear, but it probably won't be reported at all if you tell the Inspector exactly what happened. They rarely release information irrelevant to the case.' Katie didn't say anything. She didn't have to. She acknowledged what she had known all along. She would have to inform the police. And the sooner the better. The last sentence on page one of the Sevenoaks Post informed the public that an inquest would be held on Monday, March the 30th.

* * *

Inspector Dartmouth of the Barnley C.I.D. was not at all Katie's idea of a policeman. A well-cut suit in subtle checks, a Magdalene tie and highly polished brogues provided the first surprise. The second was the slow pleasant voice and sleepy eyes which belied the mobile face and ironic mouth. All this was topped by a head of naturally curly fair hair. Adam Dartmouth, she later found out, hadn't come into the Force the usual way. He came down from Cambridge with a creditable degree in spite of an easy familiarity with the paddock at Newmarket, and took a long clear look at future prospects. Finally a passion for justice and a lively curiosity about the workings of the criminal mind turned his thoughts towards the C.I.D. The leisurely pace of university life was no preparation for the hard grind ahead but he had an obstinate streak which rendered him impervious to the possibility of failure and a certain flair which could bypass more routine methods. He was married to an actress called Eve Martell and they lived in a mews cottage tucked away in the centre of Barnley, a stone's throw from County Headquarters and not much more than half an hour from the West End. It suited them both admirably.

Katie wore her grey pleated skirt with a silk shirt and bottle-green velvet jacket, the same shade as her soft suede ankle boots. She didn't consciously plan an outfit suitable for visiting a police station but confidence was a useful weapon. Adam Dartmouth looked at her approvingly. Without any inclination towards unfaithfulness, he liked the company of beautiful women, and Mrs. Rees-Williams was as pleasantly alien to the functional pine and the echoing corridors of the Barnley C.I.D. section as champagne for breakfast. He got up when she was ushered into his office. The constable retired, closing the door behind him. He offered her a chair. 'You have some information about the Tolworthy case, I believe?' he said.

'It's more a matter of elimination', answered Katie, 'and I hope you will treat what I'm going to tell you as confidential?'

'You'll have to leave me to be the judge of that,' said Adam equably. 'But there will be no record of this conversation. No ... ' he saw her glance around ... 'no tape recorders, no hidden listeners. And unless your information has a bearing on the case, your name need not be mentioned.'

Katie relaxed. This was even better than she had dared to hope. She took her folded copy of the Sevenoaks Post out of her shoulder bag and passed it, front page uppermost, across the desk.

'Don't tell me,' said the Inspector, 'that you are the mystery woman.'

Driving over to Barnley, Katie had considered how much she could safely tell. Or, to be more precise, how little she could get away with. Choosing the latter course, she related her accidental meeting with Miss Tolworthy at the Sennock Arms and explained, as she had to her mother, her choice of words during the conversation which had followed. As she spoke, she realised how thin her story sounded, how full of holes it was. Inspector Dartmouth listened without interrupting. Then he methodically exposed the inconsistencies.

'You admit that it was you who made the first approach?'

'Yes.'

'Because you recognised the name when Mrs. Ridley addressed her as Miss Tolworthy?'

'Yes.'

'Why did you not go over to the table then?'

'Because — because I didn't want to intrude.'

'You mean you wished your conversation to be private, don't you? You said that Mrs. Margaret Tolworthy was a friend of yours. One would therefore expect your meeting with her sister-in-law to be a friendly one. Yet, having invited yourself over to her table and accepted a drink, you exchanged acrimonious words and finally gave a false name. I think that requires some elucidation, Mrs. Rees-Williams.'

Katie looked back at him. So it would have to be plan one after all. 'It's a long story and I know it would bore you,' she began.

'Try me,' he invited. Katie took a deep breath and chose her words with care.

'There was an outbreak of poison-pen letters in Niederdorf — that's in Germany — last year. I — mistakenly, as it happened — tried to clear it up myself. Margaret Tolworthy was also involved. It's not too much to say that everyone suspected everyone else. When I ran into Miss Tolworthy that day, I took the opportunity of getting to know something of Margaret's background. Miss Tolworthy and I just didn't get on. That's all there was to it. As I was leaving, she asked me for my name. Naturally I didn't want Margaret to know I had been intervening. So I said the first name that came into my head. The Gloucestershire bit was an embellishment but I was thoroughly mad by then.' She realised that she could have phrased her reactions rather better. 'Not mad enough to inflict bodily harm,' she qualified. Adam Dartmouth looked amused but it didn't show in his voice.

'Did you ever visit her house?' he asked.

'Only once. She gave a cocktail party when the Brigadier and his wife were staying with her. She invited me and my mother.'

'Surely she recognised Mrs. Ponsonby-Fitzwilliam?'

'It's amazing what a little make-up can do,' murmured Katie.

'Was that the last time you saw her?'

'Yes. That was three weeks before she died.'

The Inspector glanced down at a file on the desk.

'What impressions of Mrs. Ridley did you get that day in the pub?'

'It was all rather fleeting.' Katie thought back. 'I remember a plumpish, middle-aged blonde. She didn't look happy. I got the feeling that Miss Tolworthy enjoyed making other people miserable. Especially,' she added with a flash of insight, 'those she regarded as her social inferiors.'

'I see.' Adam Dartmouth made a note, then got to his feet. 'I don't think it will be necessary to identify you as the mystery woman, Mrs. Rees-Williams. But I would like you to attend the inquest in case the coroner should require you to give evidence as to the relations between Miss Tolworthy and Mrs. Ridley.'

5

The coroner's court at Barnley in the county of Kent was held in a church hall as its usual premises were being redecorated. There was a trestle table on a dais for the coroner and a smaller one for the clerk of the court. The seven jurors — five men and two women — were allocated faded upholstery, but the public sat on hard chairs normally used for parish meetings and cosy lectures. There was a faint smell of damp clothing and ancient teaurns. Motes of dust danced in shafts of sunlight falling through slatted windows. Brief showers darkened the already sombre room. Katie, secure in corduroy basher cap and outsize dark glasses, sat in shadow near the back and fervently hoped she would be allowed to stay there.

Evidence of identification of the

deceased was given by Brigadier Henry Tolworthy. Katie hadn't noticed him when she came in — chiefly, she supposed, because she had been concentrating so hard on being invisible. So it was with a small shock of surprise that she saw him rise to his feet. He looked different, somebody she hardly knew, and she realised it was the first time she had seen him out of his own environment. In his Army quarter, at cocktail parties, striding across the playing fields, he had always smiled when they met. This solemn little man in a dark grey suit was a stranger. He identified the body as that of his sister, Eleanor Myrtle Tolworthy, and hesitated, as if wondering how on earth that second christian name had found its way onto the family tree.

'You and your family were her only living relatives?' enquired the coroner. Mr. Hardwick approved of Service witnesses. They invariably answered questions with clarity and economy.

'Myself, my wife, son and daughter,'

answered Henry Tolworthy.

'You have come over from Germany for this inquest?'

'Yes'

'When did you last see your sister alive?'

'Just over three weeks ago.'

'Thank you.' The witness was turning away. 'Oh, just a moment . . . I see by my notes that you were in England the night your sister was murdered. Why did you not mention this fact?'

There was a slight rustle of excitement at this first hint of drama. But if the Brigadier was disconcerted, his face gave nothing away.

'In the army,' he said drily, 'one learns never to volunteer information.'

'Quite.' The coroner was equally laconic. 'Where did you stay the night of Wednesday, March the twenty-fifth?'

'At my club — the Artillery.'

'You did not get in touch with your sister?'

'No. I came over for one reason, to visit my son at Sandhurst.'

'Your wife and daughter remained in Germany? Thank you, Brigadier.' When he sat down again, Katie gazed at the thinning hair on the back of his head. Something he had said didn't ring true, but the impression was so fleeting she couldn't pin it down. From the subdued muttering around her, she gathered that the public considered at least one more question should have been asked. Miss Tolworthy was reputed to be a wealthy woman. How much did her brother hope to inherit?

* * *

The next witness was Mrs. Palfrey. Katie had had a private bet that Mrs. P. would make the most of the occasion, and she wasn't wrong. From the note of quiet satisfaction in which she agreed, yes, she was Mrs. Sarah Palfrey to her last lingering syllable as she answered the coroner's final question, this was undoubtedly her finest hour. It was probably, thought Katie, the lack of ostentation which made the performance the more impressive. Sturdily built, with red cheeks and neat black hair, dressed in a chain store skirt and jacket, she stood and beamed all round the court. The coroner, well versed in the idiosyncrasies of witnesses, decided to let this one tell her story in her own words.

'Will you tell the jury how you happened to discover the body?' he invited.

'Well . . . ' The invitation was accepted. 'I came at eight, like I always do. I have the extra back-door key. I didn't even have one of them premonitions. I went into the kitchen and put on the kettle. Then I noticed that the light was on in the hall. Miss Tolworthy always turned it off before she went to bed.' Mrs. Palfrey was quite still, frowning a little, re-living the moment she had stepped out of the familiar safety of the kitchen. 'I always draw the curtains back first thing. I turned off the hall light and opened the drawing-room door. I could see by the daylight coming through. The drawers of the desk were all pulled out and there were books on the floor and papers everywhere. Then I saw a shoe . . . ' Involuntarily she shivered. The sunlight outside was expunged as if by a giant hand. Someone suppressed a scream.

'I had to pass the end of the sofa to open the curtains. I thought she was asleep at first. That is, till I saw her face and that pink scarf of hers, knotted round her neck.' There was a pause. Sarah Palfrey seemed to come back from a long way. 'Then', she said briskly, 'I screamed. Not that that did any good. There was no one to hear. So I telephoned the police.'

'That seems very clear, Mrs. Palfrey. What happened next?'

'I made myself a cup of tea. I could have done with something stronger but she kept it all locked up.' Tension relaxed. People shifted on the hard seats. The coroner went smoothly on to the next question.

'How did you get on with your employer?' He had never met Miss Tolworthy but his wife had once partnered her at bridge and reported that she won as malevolently as she lost. Sarah Palfrey answered the question in her own way.

'It's a seller's market,' she said simply. Just as if she had spent most of her adult life treading the marble floors of the Stock Exchange.

'You mean that competent household staff are hard to find,' translated Mr. Hardwick for the benefit of the jury. That was just what his wife had been pointing out for years.

'Miss Tolworthy knew I wouldn't stay there if there was any nastiness,' said Mrs. Palfrey and clumped solidly back to her seat. Somehow that last sentence illustrated the dead woman's character more clearly than any detailed biography.

James Hardwick's thoughts about Sarah Palfrey were taking a different line. There was only her word for what had happened. He didn't doubt that she had told the truth about the discovery of the body, but was that the first time she had returned to the house since her previous day's employment there? Could Miss Tolworthy have had a hold over her? Mrs. Palfrey was a proud woman. She was also strong and well-muscled. And she had a key to the back door.

★   ★   ★

Chief Inspector Dartmouth's evidence was short and to the point. The 999 call had been received at Barnley Police Station at 8.12 on the morning of March the twenty-sixth. He and Sergeant Wills had reached 'Little Sandhurst' shortly before nine o'clock, and had been joined by the police surgeon. Cause of death was mechanical strangulation, time of death approximately between nine and eleven the night before. The deceased had been sitting on the sofa and her assailant had attacked from behind. There was as yet no explanation for the ransacking of the drawing-room. Enquiries were proceeding. The coroner asked few questions. The last, however, was the one the whole court had been waiting for. 'I understand that you have located the so-called Mrs. Ponsonby-Fitzwilliam?'

'She came to see me of her own accord. I am quite satisfied that she has nothing to do with this case.' He knew that the coroner had his statement to this effect, but these things had to be aired. Sensing universal disappointment, he added with — as it seemed to the person to whom it was directed — a rueful shrug. 'She is here today in case anything she knows should become relevant in the course of this hearing.'

Only then did Katie realise she had made a fundamental mistake. Most of the spectators here were local and many of them knew each other by sight. One could, however, have merged by being inconspicuously dressed. The sky-blue cap and, above all, the outsize dark glasses immediately marked her out as an alien. In order to avoid recognition by Mrs. Ridley, she had succeeded in attracting attention from everyone else. She did the only possible thing. She looked round the faces as every other member of the public was doing, even removing her glasses to peer into the darker corners. Interest was finally focussed on a willowy ash-blonde who had only come in to get out of the rain and whose thoughts were concentrated solely on an invitation to Benidorm. The court resumed. Mrs. Ridley was called to the stand.

* * *

She was as Katie had remembered her — plump, fiftyish and fussily dressed. This time she was also clanking with costume jewellery. It was soon clear that she had been called because she appeared to have been the last person to see Miss Tolworthy alive. 'It was about four o'clock on the Wednesday afternoon,' she said reluctantly. She hadn't wanted to give evidence at all but a neighbour had seen her turn into the driveway of 'Little Sandhurst' and neighbours didn't forget things like that.

'Did you often exchange visits?'

'We occasionally had a cup of coffee or a drink together.' Mrs. Ridley paused. 'She wasn't easy to get on with.' Seeing the way things were going, she had sense enough to admit to an uneasy relationship. It seemed to her that anyone claiming friendship with the late Eleanor would automatically be suspected of perjury. Even the Brigadier, from what she'd heard, had had little affection for his only sister.

'Why did you continue to see her?' asked the coroner reasonably.

'It would have seemed unneighbourly . . . '

'Did you stay long that afternoon?'

'Not really. I only called to return a

book. She was listening to the news on the radio — I think an acquaintance of hers had just been rescued in Snowdonia — so I came away.'

'Did she seem as usual that day?' asked the corner. Mrs. Ridley smiled faintly. 'Just as usual,' she answered.

The Inspector remembered the last-minute rescue on Snowdon. Briefly he recalled the dramatic details. Then he forgot about it. He waited to hear the verdict which he considered a foregone conclusion. It couldn't be accident: suicide unlikely in the extreme. That left murder. He collected his sergeant and drove back to headquarters. Several interesting points had emerged from the inquest and the sooner he got down to following them up, the sooner he could piece together the relevant facts and get down to the really fascinating part of the puzzle — the psychological angle.

★　★　★

The crime reporter of the Sevenoaks Post felt that the police had let him down. Having been presented with the mystery woman on a plate, what had they done about it? For heaven's sake, they hadn't even found her! And when she had very conveniently turned up and made a statement, they hadn't called her as a witness. Well, now that he knew she was in court he was going to track her down and follow her home. Once he'd got her real name, he could do a background feature for next Saturday's issue. He definitely needed some interim material to keep public interest alive. Outside the hall he hesitated. The ash-blonde moved off first, so he decided to take a chance and follow her. Katie, seeing that Brigadier Tolworthy was talking to a couple of women she didn't know, was more than pleased to be able to walk away unrecognised. Henry Tolworthy hadn't seen her in court: better leave it that way.

'Don't look now,' said a voice behind

her, 'but the Press will shortly find out it's pursuing the wrong woman. How about a drink?' Slowly she turned round. 'I'm Bill Ridley,' he added, 'and that is my car over there.'

He drove her back to Sevenoaks very fast. Katie, who had come over by bus to avoid Barnley's parking problems, relaxed and listened to him talk. Bill Ridley, according to himself, had no pretensions that smacked of culture or the intellect. He was simply a man who intended to go faster than any of his contemporaries in a Formula I racing car.

'That is going to take some time,' he explained as they sat together at the bar of the Mitre. 'Incidentally, why don't you take those goggles off?' Katie removed her cap as well and shook the smooth sweep of black hair across her forehead. 'I suppose you wouldn't hang around Brands Hatch the next time there's a big race?' he said hopefully. 'I could do with a personal bit of glamour in the pits.' Katie laughed. Relief from tension made her feel lightheaded. Also, she'd never before met anyone quite like this dedicated driver. He was probably in his late twenties, with a nose which had once been broken, a windburnt face and hazel eyes which concentrated on everything he said and did. 'I started in Formula Three,' he told her, 'and was lucky to survive a particularly slaphappy lot. So I used all my resources scraping up enough money to buy my way into Formula Two. Even Miss Tolworthy came up with a loan, my mother told me. But it's the next step that's the important one. If I can't find a sponsor, I'll probably sign a long-term contract — if one of the big boys offers me one.' He finished his tomato juice. 'To coin a phrase, I never drink before driving. When can I see you again? I usually stay with Mum when I'm in England but don't be put off by that. Your secret is safe with me. I shall now drive you home so that I'll know where to pick you up again next time.'

Katie, still amused, waved him off to an accelerating roar. She didn't think she had contributed more than a dozen sentences, and monosyllabic at that. But she found Bill's single-minded attitude refreshingly uncomplicated and she would see him again. There were two things, though, that she couldn't understand: one was Miss Tolworthy's reputed loan to a man with whom she had no ties of relationship or mutual interests and no guarantee of financial reward — and the second was the curiously subservient attitude of Mrs. Ridley to the late unlamented Eleanor. It didn't add up. She wasn't to know that if she had carried that train of thought a bit further, she could have come up with the solution. But not in time to avert another fatality.

6

Wednesday was a day full of promise. To begin with, it was April the first and the sun was shining. The first mail brought her passport duly stamped with an American visa, and an airmail letter from Washington. Bill phoned and announced he was driving to London and proposed to give her lunch at a pub on the river. Her mother won a fifty-pound premium bond prize and found a teacher volunteering to help in the kindergarten before going abroad. Even the children were angelic.

Bill was wearing charcoal grey. 'My executive suiting,' he explained.

'If you'd only worn your frilly-fronted shirt,' pointed out Katie, sliding in beside him, 'we'd be identical.' The hood of the old Aston Martin was down to celebrate spring. 'Heaven! I've always wanted an open car.'

'I've never wanted a passenger before,' he said. He had a disconcerting honesty which left her momentarily speechless. Not an enigmatic man but certainly an unusual one.

'This is the first audition I've ever had to attend.' He manoeuvred expertly through the Sevenoaks morning traffic. 'Well, I suppose you'd call it an interview. The Chobham team is looking out for drivers and phoned me to come along and tell them just how good I am.'

'Oh Bill, that's marvellous! I knew this was going to be a special day.'

Bill dropped her off in Piccadilly and told her he'd pick her up outside the Ritz in two hours' time. Happily aware that there was nothing else she had to do, she wandered into St. James's Park, along the paths, over the grass and into the sea of daffodils opposite Birdcage Walk. As she went, she thought about Rhodri's letter. It had been short as always but hopeful. A colleague was returning to England in a month's time and Rhodri had an option on the house he was vacating. It was small and painted white and there was a magnolia tree in the back yard. He'd let her know, he wrote.

What's another month when there's all the time in the world? Time to plan a wardrobe, sell the car, spring-clean the flat, see the apple orchards in blossom . . . Katie planned haphazardly as she retraced her footsteps. Maybe she'd buy a hat right now, the sort of hat that was in keeping with the mood of the day — something feminine, something absurd, something concocted from spindrift and froth. There must be hat-shops within a couple of hundred yards. It was quite by chance that she left the park by another gate. She stood on the pavement and looked across the stream of cars and buses to the other side. The houses of Piccadilly marched up towards Hyde Park Corner. Exactly opposite her was the Artillery Club.

★ ★ ★

Funny, thought Katie, how the Tolworthys kept cropping up. Just when they had been neatly pigeonholed, something slightly off-beat would happen and she would be driven to examine their life-style all over again. She remembered now what had, to her ears, sounded wrong in the evidence the Brigadier had given at the inquest. The Artillery was not a residential club. She recalled that Patrick had once passed on that, until now, useless piece of information. So Henry Tolworthy had either been surprised into providing himself with a false alibi or he had been confident enough to assume that his statement would be taken at face value. There could, of course, be a second line of defence. He could have spent the night of Wednesday, March the twenty-fifth with someone whom he did not wish to involve unless absolutely necessary. Anyway, she reminded herself, it was none of her business. She was just turning away when a figure emerged from the portals of the Artillery Club and stood at the top of the steps. For once there was a gap in the traffic. Brigadier Tolworthy advanced with the relentless momentum of a tank. 'Katie Rees-Williams!' He said. 'What an unexpected pleasure. I think you have some explaining to do, my dear. They make very good coffee at my club . . . '

The Ladies' Room was obviously a grudging concession to changing standards. It was small and dark and overlooked a bleak courtyard at the back of the house. But the coffee was excellent. Katie, forced into the position of defendant, nibbled at a biscuit and waited for the charge. It was unexpectedly mild.

'Why didn't you come and talk to me after the inquest?' demanded Henry Tolworthy. 'Oh yes, I saw you there, lurking behind the dark glasses. Had your hair cut too, haven't you? Suits you. Well, why did you ignore me?'

'I tried,' Katie answered truthfully, 'but you were surrounded. And then I was offered a lift by Bill Ridley. In fact, he drove me up to London today.'

'You be careful of that young man. Once he gets an idea into his head, it sticks. What would Rhodri say if he knew?'

'What would Margaret say,' retorted Katie, 'if she knew this club was non-residential?' The moment she said it, she repented. 'I'm sorry, it's nothing to do with me.' Henry Tolworthy grinned and immediately shed ten years.

'I didn't expect the statement to be questioned — not unless I was suspected of murdering my sister. Oh, I know the motive is there — the bulk of her estate comes to me — and I've never liked her. But I would never have risked my freedom, nor would I have been foolish enough to give a false alibi. I did come over to see my son who needed urgent advice. What I did after that I have no intention of revealing, least of all to Margaret.'

Katie smiled back and got to her feet. 'Thank you for the coffee. Bill's taking me to lunch by the river, so I really must go.' He accompanied her through the hall.

'Still mad about racing?'

'Oh yes. Did you know that your sister put up part of the purchase money for the Formula Two car?'

'Did she indeed!' The Brigadier's face was grim. 'I wonder what form of interest was extorted in that particular transaction?'

The tide was flowing strongly upriver. Two eights powered smoothly past, a length apart, blades flashing in the sunlight. A solitary sail tacked bravely across the little waves. Bill thankfully shed his executive jacket and leant on the parapet.

'What a wonderful world!' A contract to drive a Chobham was his for the taking. Champagne frothed into two glasses. The breeze lifted Katie's hair like feathers across her forehead. He leaned forward and kissed her gently on the mouth. This, he thought, was a moment he would remember all his life. He photographed it in the memory which, he was supremely confident, would one day record his first world championship victory. 'Monza, do you think? Or Zandvoort? I think I'd prefer it to be Silverstone.'

Katie smiled across the bubbles which tickled her nose. This was Bill's day. She wouldn't spoil it by referring to Henry Tolworthy's last — and most disturbing — words. The expedition ended as lightheartedly as it had begun. 'If you ever need a fan with a stopwatch,' offered Katie, 'nobody miscounts figures like me.'

'I might just take you up on that,' answered Bill, 'at the American Grand Prix.'

★ ★ ★

The crime reporter came up with a new angle in his bath on Thursday morning and reckoned he might, he just might, have another scoop if he could get official sanction before time of going to press. He decided to miss breakfast. He arrived in Barnley while Adam Dartmouth was grilling mushrooms and was hanging round C.I.D. headquarters when the Inspector arrived to begin the day's work. While waiting, he had had time to put a call through to the B.B.C. in London.

Adam had reservations concerning the methods sometimes employed by journalists but he admired initiative. He looked at the thin, cynical face opposite him and wondered how far its owner would get in Fleet Street. The reporter guessed his thoughts. 'I'm quite a big fish in my particular pond.' He smiled, wryly. 'Too much competition elsewhere. Anyway, what I came to see you about is this. I think I know who killed Miss Tolworthy.'

'That,' said the Inspector gently, 'is very interesting, because so do I. So far, however, there is no proof.'

'If I can provide that, do I get the scoop?'

'When do you go to press? Tomorrow? It depends entirely, as you know, when an arrest is made. But I'll do what I can for you. Now, tell me who you think did it and your reasons for coming to that conclusion.'

Other people too were forming conclusions. Katie started off from the last words Brigadier Tolworthy had spoken to her. Miss Tolworthy drove a hard bargain. Why, then, had she so uncharacteristically invested money in that most insecure of assets, a racing car? Had Henry Tolworthy known about it in spite of his implied denial? She speculated as to his reactions if he began to suspect that his sister's grip on her finances was beginning to slide. From various remarks made by Margaret during desultory golf course conversations, Katie had gathered that retirement from the army would only be made bearable by eventual inheritance of the much older Eleanor's estate. 'Can you see us in a bungalow at Bognor? It isn't that we've got expensive tastes — it's just that Henry has always been used to space. Oh, there's no question of our sharing 'Little Sandhurst' (typical, isn't it?) with her because that would never work. But by the terms of the old General's will, a certain sum comes to us the day Henry leaves the army, and eventually the residue'. Margaret hadn't put all that into one sentence but it had been a recurring theme interspersing the perfunctory 'good shot!' and the more frequent commiseration. Katie, keeping an alert eye on eight five-year-olds running amok with poster paints, brought her thoughts back to Eleanor. She wished she knew the sum involved. It certainly couldn't have been small as Bill, presumably with his mother's help as well, had been able to buy his Formula II car. Obviously there must have been strings attached — strings more familiarly known as interest rates. Miss Tolworthy wasn't likely to go around tossing banknotes like nuts in May. The more she considered the way her thoughts were leading, the less she liked it. She could, of course, be wrong.

But her theory did at least explain the disorder in the drawing-room.

Bill Ridley had been indulging in a, for him, most unusual occupation — introspection. He very rarely looked back because all his ambitions were concerned with the future. Even as a child he had been fascinated by cars. Now they were his whole life. He knew that he was a good racing driver. He also knew that talent was not enough. Even talent and the right backing did not necessarily add up to success on the circuit. The vital element that he himself had was instantaneous communication between brain and machine. His mind became completely attuned, his concentration total. None of this had to be put into words. What did need to be considered was the conditions of purchase of his present Formula II car. He had never really known Miss Tolworthy but the Brigadier and family had been fairly frequent visitors when stationed in England, and he had been invited when John and

Jane were around. They were, of course, younger than he, and it was their father with whom he'd formed a temporary bond. Partly because his own father, the not over-lamented Councillor Ridley, had died not long after acquiring what he would have described as a most desirable property next door to 'Little Sandhurst', and partly through a certain straightforward similarity of outlook. He wondered now if the Brigadier had known about the loan and, if so, what his reaction had been. It was part of the estate which would come to him after all. Bill also wondered for the first time — till now he had merely been unquestioningly thankful — the reasons behind Miss Tolworthy's loan; and the more he thought, the less he liked what he saw. The most chilling factor was the notion that repayment had been of far more importance than the original transaction.

★   ★   ★

'It was the rescue on Snowdon, of course,' Adam Dartmouth told his wife afterwards. He didn't discuss all his cases with her, only those in which he knew she'd be interested or when he reckoned her opinion would be valuable. Eve, as an actress, had a highly individual way of looking at people. 'What was?' she asked. Adam hadn't chosen the most convenient moment because she was just beginning to get inside the skin of her new part.

'Put that script down and have a drink with me. Come on, love.' He poured out a couple of very dry martinis. 'You know — the Tolworthy case. It was the reporter, I admit, who came up with that angle and he earned himself his scoop. He'll probably be editor one day. Bright lad. Anyway . . . ' he raised his glass . . . 'I need to talk about it now it's over. The final stages I sometimes find hard to take, especially when one's sympathies are not on the side of the victim.' He paused and drank.

'How did Snowdon come into it?' Eve asked practically. She knew that Adam suffered vicariously and she could sympathise, but she also knew that the best form of therapy was talking about the mechanics of the case.

'Well, the son of one of Miss Tolworthy's army chums got caught in a blizzard near the top of the mountain and had to dig himself into the snow to survive. By the time visibility returned, he was suffering from frostbite and exposure. The moment of his rescue is not relevant — the time of its release as a news item *is*. That was at nine o'clock on the evening Miss Tolworthy died. It had not been announced before that time; the crime reporter checked with the B.B.C. Mrs. Ridley stated at the inquest that Miss Tolworthy had been listening to the radio at four o'clock and news of the rescue was coming through then. It's an interesting psychological point that she could have heard it at home herself at nine o'clock but the association of ideas, i.e. Miss

Tolworthy listening and commenting, gave her away. She wouldn't have paid much attention by herself because she didn't personally know the man who had been saved.'

'So Mrs. Ridley didn't go up to the house at four o'clock?'

'No. She decided to wait for dark. She probably arrived when Miss Tolworthy actually was listening to the nine o'clock news, her TV set being out of order.'

'The reasoning sounds a little specious to me,' Eve said doubtfully, 'but presumably it turned out that you were right.'

'I don't think for a moment that she had murder in mind but she had screwed up her courage to the point at which anything might happen.' He got up and started pacing round the room. 'As you've probably guessed, Miss Tolworthy had decided to foreclose. Either raise the cash or sell the car.'

Neither of the Dartmouths knew Bill Ridley except as a name connected with motor racing, but both had sufficient imagination to guess what that loss was going to mean to him. The only other person who knew was his mother, and she blamed herself entirely. She was the one who had grasped so eagerly at the proffered loan, she the only one who could have foreseen an ulterior motive behind Eleanor Tolworthy's falsely gracious smile.

'You mean,' said Eve incredulously, 'that she only lent the money so as to withdraw it when that withdrawal could cause the most misery?'

'That's exactly what I mean. Mrs. Ridley couldn't believe it either. So she went to plead with her so-called friend. She didn't expect mercy and she didn't receive it. I think she killed in a moment of blind fury. Then she ransacked the desk and cabinets till she found the damning I.O.U. It was a cash transaction, you see. That piece of paper was the only evidence. Incidentally, we found her fingerprints on letters and documents scattered all over the floor. If she'd tidied everything away instead of panic flight . . . '

'Poor woman,' said Eve. She couldn't help thinking that the whole story would transfer admirably to the stage but that didn't make her sympathy any the less genuine. 'I suppose she did that hovering act at the pub in a desperate hope of discovering that the stranger had some sort of hold over the feared and distrusted Eleanor?'

'Just as,' agreed Adam, 'her last desperate hope of avoiding attention was to focus it on the mystery woman. I still blame myself bitterly for at least one unnecessary death.' Eve decided the time had come to close the file.

'You couldn't possibly', she pointed out, 'have got there in time.'

★　★　★

Bill Ridley had lived for twenty-seven years before he found out what his mother meant to him. She had always been there in the background, standing

233

up for him when his father had, for example, wanted him to take up riding instead of tinkering about with infernal engines. Gymkhanas provided, to the aspiring Councillor, an entrée to a different world. Since he became a racing driver, she had invariably been there for early morning starts and unexpected returns, silently encouraging, ready to listen. Maybe not very clever, certainly lacking in judgment, but on his side without reservation. In one blinding moment he realised all she had done for him — the moment he found the I.O.U. she had been unable to bring herself to throw away. Somehow his mother, with her own brand of logic, had reasoned that as long as she had the piece of paper, nobody could prove that she owed the money. He also realised that the police could not be far behind. He couldn't allow her to be arrested, not someone who feared confined spaces as she did. The Formula II car which had been so dearly bought was still at Brands Hatch.

His treasured old Aston Martin was outside the front door. 'Let's go out for a drink, Mum,' he said and carefully fastened her seat-belt. There was a long straight stretch of road, with a left-hand turn just in front of a venerable and spreading oak. Bill pressed his foot hard on the accelerator. He'd had plenty of experience of jumping free at the last moment. But for the first and last time in his life, he miscalculated. They both died instantaneously.

7

When she eventually traced the whole business back to the beginning, Katie realised that each link in the chain had led irrevocably to the next. Henry Tolworthy's visit to England provided yet another. When, out of the blue, he telephoned Katie and invited her to return with him to Germany and stay a few days, she accepted without hesitation. Partly it was the need to get away after Bill's heroic gesture, partly because she was genuinely interested in the Tolworthy family and would like to see the Fordyns again. There was also at the back of her mind the unfinished business of the poison-pen letters. It was all very well to come to a conclusion, something else to take action. If Barney Fordyn really was responsible, his parents would have to do something about him and his future.

A third reason was that her own life was at a standstill, past cut off, future still over the horizon. She wanted to get away. As an odd postscript to her decision, she found out that morning that the teacher waiting to go abroad had in fact been accepted by one of the army schools at Niederdorf. 'I had an interview with the headmaster, Mr. Grey,' she told Katie, 'and he approved my qualifications. He told me about his divorce. It's not so easy when the wife is German, is it?'

It was late Sunday morning when they reached Niederdorf. Church bells rang as they bowled across Holland and April showers caught the flails of the wayside windmill. The camp, thought Katie, looked exactly the same except that the trees were higher. She half-recognised a face or two as people in cars swept by on their way to pre-lunch drinks or Mess lunches. Henry, it appeared, knew everybody. He had been an easy companion on the journey, not voluble but experienced in the art of gentle entertaining. Margaret was welcoming and Katie genuinely glad to see her, but the nicest surprise of all was that Jane, Hans and Gaby were spending the day at the house beside the forest.

'Reconciliation!' said Margaret happily. 'John talked Henry round the last time he went to Sandhurst. But Henry's been so much more tolerant recently. I think it's your influence, my dear. Now, give us Rhodri's latest news. When do you hope to join him?'

Later that day, Katie finally solved something she had purposely pushed to the back of her mind but never forgotten. Looking out at the trees which seemed to move together in the gathering dusk, she suddenly asked the question she could never have asked her husband.

'Did you ever see Rhodri down in the woods last summer? I had the impression he was meeting someone there.'

'He was indeed,' answered Henry Tolworthy. 'On one occasion at least he was meeting me. We used to have army exercises to test individual reactions. Other personnel — such as Rhodri — trained in surveillance were brought in to follow our men and hope to remain undetected.'

'And was the signal,' Katie said slowly, 'a telephone call with no word spoken?'

'That's right. There were Dutch, Belgians and Germans involved and any word could have betrayed an accent. It was all part of the set-up. We do it every few months. There's a grandstand view from here, as you can imagine. Other people, of course, get accidentally involved. I think Margaret saw you out there one evening . . .'

'What a pity,' Katie said sincerely, 'that I didn't know then what was going on.'

★ ★ ★

At that moment Barney Fordyn was reluctantly, but with a sense of duty to be performed, sitting down to compose a letter to Mrs. Rees-Williams. He cleared a space on his desk by the simple expedient of sweeping what was on it to the floor, tore a sheet of paper off a pad, took up a pen in his left hand and started to write. An hour and three drafts later, he admitted defeat. It wasn't that he didn't know what he wanted to say. It was just that too much was at stake and he might do incalculable harm. And he wasn't even certain of his facts. The story he'd been told could have been slanted. He threw down the pen and went over to the door. 'Nearly supper-time, Mum?' he shouted down the stairs.

Astonishingly, at supper he found that his troubles were over. Well, not exactly over — but things had definitely been made easier.

'I hear that Katie Rees-Williams is staying with the Tolworthys,' Claire remarked, handing round plates of bacon and sausages.

'Really?!' Barney couldn't hide his

pleasure. Claire and Mark exchanged a rueful glance. Was their son showing an interest in older women? Katie was very attractive but not the type to be more than disinterestedly kind to schoolboys. 'How long is she staying?'

'Till Wednesday, I think. We might have them to dinner on Tuesday if they're free — don't you think, Mark?' Mark agreed with a certain amount of enthusiasm. He liked Katie too, though he'd never thought of her in terms of more than casual friendship. Fortunately for everyone concerned, he admitted to himself . . . They're behaving, thought Barney with sudden surprise, like a normal married couple; maybe there's hope after all.

That evening, after Jane and Hans had departed with a beguilingly sleepy Gaby, Katie decided that the time had come to bring everything out into the open, especially as they had been invited to dine with the Fordyns on Tuesday. There had been too much suspicion, far too many misunderstandings — and the case had gone on much too long. Now that she had all the clues in her possession, this was the time to test her conclusions. Sitting round the open fire after supper, she outlined the indictments she had assembled against Claire and Veronica and explained how each one had failed. 'I even suspected you, Margaret,' she said with a smile, 'till I came to this house and realised it just wasn't in character.'

'I can remember the exact moment', said Margaret drily.

'Was I really that transparent?'

'You were positively vibrating with zeal. You really burned to clear it up, didn't you? Because of Rhodri?'

'Yes.' Katie thought briefly of trying to explain and elected not to risk embarrassing her hosts with personal revelations.

'Then I thought of Barney,' she said slowly.

★ ★ ★

After breakfast next morning, Katie and Henry Tolworthy set off for the small town of Arnsbrueck. Sitting side by side in the back of an army car ('It's time I paid them an official visit'), they talked little as the driver manoeuvred competently up the autobahn. As they ran into the Sauerland the countryside changed. Smudges on the horizon turned into hills. Not mountains but sizeable, even skiable, hills. Katie amused herself working out the line she would take from each summit.

'Did you ever ski?' she asked Henry.

'What, risk my future on two pieces of wood on a gradient of one in three? Not bloody likely!'

When they reached Arnsbrueck, a pleasant little town set on wooded slopes above the river, Katie asked to be dropped off in the Marktplatz and arranged to be picked up at the same place at four o'clock. The car swept away and she was left on her own. For a moment she stood there, looking about her. She'd been so pleased at the ease with which her path had been smoothed that she had overlooked anything so prosaic as a plan. She studied the various arrows indicating places of interest and then made for the only source of information she could think of. She had no difficulty in finding Brigade Headquarters which was signposted for the benefit of the lower IQs. She could, she supposed, have come in with Henry but for this particular mission it was better to be on her own. She produced her passport and said she wanted to visit the employment office. The corporal on the gate gave her a temporary pass and an escort and said how about a cup of char at the NAAFI Club when he came off duty. Katie declined regretfully: thirsty as she was, time was getting on. Taken along at a brisk trot, she tried to rehearse her opening gambit. Tracy Symonds, the schoolteacher still at Vine Court Road, had amassed an astonishing amount of information when she had come over to Niederdorf for interview. Among other things, she had mentioned that Lindy Grey's mother had formerly been employed as a clerk at Arnsbrueck and it was there she had met John Grey, then head of the army school. Her surname, someone had suggested, was one she had probably been happy to change.

Ushered into the office, Katie found to her relief that she was the only client. She told the middle-aged woman behind the desk that close friends were likely to be posted to Arnsbrueck in the near future (no one could disprove a statement as vague as that) and what were their chances of obtaining the services of a *Putzfrau*? The woman looked back without interest and said she hadn't had one on her books for months. The new paper factory in the town paid much better wages and who could blame them? She added that she herself would be off to the factory at the drop of a hat if she could get a German work permit, and how one was supposed to exist, let alone have a decent standard of living on what she was getting . . . Katie let her chunter on for a bit and then asked what she had come to find out. She had a friend, she said, who had once worked in this headquarters and, as she was passing through, she'd like to call on her parents. Could she possibly have Anna Guggenheimer's home address? Miss Bewley, whose name she could now see on a placard on the desk, levered herself over to the filing cabinets.

'Guggenheimer? I seem to remember the name.' She extracted a thin cardboard folder. 'Of course! She married Mr. Grey, didn't she? Caused quite a stir at the time.'

'Clerks who marry headmasters don't grow on trees,' Katie encouraged.

'Very true. I never thought her quite the type . . . ' Miss Bewley paused, obviously not quite sure how close a friend Katie was.

'Exactly,' agreed Katie. Now they knew where they were. 'She worked here for about five years?'

'Oh, there was nothing against her ability . . . ' Another pause, even more pregnant. Katie knew she ought to be feeling bad about the shameless way in which she was manipulating the woman opposite her but she could work up no sympathy at all for Miss Bewley. Unfortunately her impatience must have showed because the temperature dropped by several degrees. Gone was the sly hint of girlish confidences.

'The address is Bismarckstrasse 7/21,' she said briskly and snapped the folder shut.

Katie cursed herself. Would she never learn?

'I'm sorry to take up so much of your time,' she said apologetically, 'but I've been out of touch with Anna for some years and I wondered if you'd seen her recently? Is she still very pretty?' That was a stab in the dark but immediately Katie knew she was on to something. Miss Bewley settled back in her chair, choosing her words with relish.

'Yes indeed. Much too pretty for her

own good. Blonde curls and those china-blue eyes . . . How poor Mr. Grey was taken in, I'll never really know.' The bun on top of her head quivered with excitement and her bulbous brown eyes hinted at untold indelicacies. 'Soldiers!' she hissed.

Back in the market square, Katie studied the buildings with more attention. One in particular held her scrutiny. It was an ordinary-looking hotel, probably one of a category found so often on the continent which let rooms most lucratively by the hour. Was that where pretty, adventurous Anna Guggenheimer had gone with her reputed lovers? The Alter Markt was alive with stalls in the spring sunshine. But all the fragrance of hyacinth and freesia could not sweeten the odour of corruption and decay she smelt when involuntarily she looked down the dark passage under that discreetly-lettered sign 'Hotel'. Maybe it came from the drains, maybe the sinister atmosphere was the effect produced by chiaroscuro.

One thing was certain. John Grey, respected headmaster, had never known about places like this. His bride must have played her hand very cleverly. Or had he found out in the end? Was that the reason for the divorce? And how old had Lindy been then? Only one person could tell her that and she wasn't yet prepared to ask Mr. Grey. In any case, the picture was already clear in her head — and the Brigadier was the one to advise her what to do. Thinking of Henry made her realise that he was lunching with colleagues and therefore she'd have to find some food for herself. What she wanted was a nice old-fashioned Bierhaus and there was one of those down a side street on the other side of the market. She rounded a drift of mimosa on the corner of a stall and came face to face with Patrick Darran.

8

For the first time in his life, Barney Fordyn insisted on attending a dinner party in his parents' house. He even brushed his hair and put on his suit. When the guests arrived punctually at seven forty-five he was there to open the door. Mark and Claire, faced at last with a presentable son, blessed the radiant Katie and agreed that maybe the older woman was going to be a factor in his future development.

The dinner party turned out to have three distinct stages. The first was predictable. The guests settled down, drinks were produced and conversation was general. Katie fought against a feeling of disorientation, brought on by seeing the Fordyns again in a house identical to the one she and Rhodri had inhabited and knowing that she would not be walking up the street again at the end of the evening. It was also odd what a difference it made being an outsider. For one thing, no one had yet seen the deceptively plain white and gold dinner dress recently bought in a Sevenoaks boutique with America in mind. For another, she was looking at the Fordyn family with eyes which had not seen them for several months. Claire looked more relaxed, Mark was noticeably less aggressive, especially towards his son, and Barney a revelation. She wondered if his room was still in its state of farcical confusion and was sure that it was. Barney hadn't changed: he was just up to something.

The second stage was reached after the Belgian pâté and veal-and-mushroom casserole had been praised and disposed of. It was Margaret Tolworthy who introduced the subject of the letters.

'Katie has a new theory,' she said casually, 'and she has discussed it with us. We'd like to know what you think of it.' Henry looked benign, Mark and

Claire slightly constrained. Barney's head came up sharply. Mark got up and replenished the wine glasses. 'We all suspected each other, of course,' went on Margaret. 'In fact, the case against Veronica was one of the more convincing. However, all that is in the past. We're concerned with the future. Claire, you remember that one of the addresses contained a continental seven?' Claire nodded. 'Did you know that Lindy Grey's mother is German?'

For a moment there was dead silence. Then everyone started talking. Everyone except Barney. Katie's was the voice of authority.

'She had a gay and pretty mother called Anna who had obviously enjoyed life in a garrison town before marriage to an older man. When the break-up came, Lindy would have been at an age to miss most desperately the mother who had deserted her, the mother who . . . ' she hesitated a moment . . . 'probably took away the sunshine.'

'Very poetic,' beamed Henry.

'She's a bright lass,' Mark put in unexpectedly, 'too bright for her environment. Such children have been known to turn to crime in search of the stimulus they fail to find at school or at home.'

'How did she get on with her father?' asked Margaret.

'She spent as little time with him as possible,' answered Claire. Little Lindy never did anything by halves. If she had loved her father before, she now hated him with equal fervour. Claire got up and put plates into the hatch. She went out to the kitchen and passed through a glass bowl of fresh fruit salad and a plateful of homemade ginger biscuits. For the next few minutes there was appreciative silence. Then Mark produced the cheese-board and conversation broke out again.

'A friend of mine,' remarked Henry to nobody in particular, 'had a manic daughter who disappeared into the squatter world, emerging infrequently only to thumb her nose at her agonised parents. Where is Lindy now, by the way?' Everyone looked at Barney. He shook his head. 'Doubtless she sees herself as a rebel against society,' went on Henry, unaware that until recently he had described his daughter in just such terms.

'That's beside the point,' said his wife. 'What Katie thinks is that it was Lindy who wrote the letters.'

★ ★ ★

The last stage was reached over coffee and liqueurs. The men didn't linger at the table, they almost immediately joined the ladies. Claire poured out coffee. Barney handed round cream and sugar.

'She could, of course, have picked up the information she needed from observation and her own contemporaries,' Margaret continued. 'Jane was originally at the same school, so almost certainly word would have got around when she and Hans decided to live together.' Henry looked embarrassed. Reconciliations were all very well and he had been delighted to see his daughter looking so happy but he still couldn't bring himself to approve. It was Mark's turn next as Margaret skated over the thin ice which covered his affaire with Joanna. 'There were rumours about that — or Barney may have speculated . . . ' Barney remained impassive. He wasn't giving anything away. 'Barney also passed on golf course gossip, such as Veronica's much publicized trials — didn't you, Barney?' This time he had to answer.

'It did seem good for a laugh,' he admitted.

'Thank you,' said Katie with half a smile. 'As for seeing me following Rhodri, one can assume she was larking about in the forest that evening last summer.' She didn't explain about the silent-tongued phone, but as she spoke she remembered the incident, practically the same situation, at Vine Court Road when Rhodri had stayed in the flat; and the explanation (though a completely different one) slid across the surface of her mind. Her mother had warned her earlier in the week that she had had one obscene and one heavy-breathing call and she, Katie, in the panic of the moment, had completely forgotten about it. Another little piece of the puzzle solved.

'Lindy was several times seen in the vicinity of the German post office,' she went on, 'but nobody paid attention to a schoolgirl — even my super sleuth Gary!'

'There's one interesting point,' said Margaret. 'Why, after posting all the other letters, did she take the risk of delivering Claire's by hand?'

'I can answer that,' interposed Mark, 'because I remember a conversation one night at supper during that week. In this case she hadn't got the money for a stamp. She had spent all her weekly allowance. So she nipped in, ostensibly to see Barney, and dropped the letter on the hall table.'

'But Barney might have mentioned seeing her,' objected Margaret.

'He wouldn't, you know. To Barney she, like Chesterton's postman, was part of the landscape.'

'She must have been there at some time during the party,' Claire put in, 'because whenever she'd had cookery class, she brought a piece of whatever she'd made, usually wrapped in silver foil, and left it for Barney.' So that, thought Katie, was the little parcel in coloured paper sitting beside the bottle of Goldener Oktober which Patrick had left for her. She could see it as clearly as if it were yesterday. And yet a lifetime seemed to have passed since then. 'There is, of course, no proof,' she said flatly. Barney, who had been listening bemusedly to the rapid crossfire of fact and fancy, heaved himself out of his abstraction.

'There is,' he said. 'She told me.'

Barney eventually made a statement, keeping it as brief as possible. 'Before she went to . . . ' he began. 'Before she went away, she said she'd done it out of boredom and frustration. She said it got a bit scary after Joanna . . . Whether she told me to show off how clever she'd been or whether in case someone else was accused, I don't know.' He managed a grin. 'Probably the former. Anyway, I promised not to say anything. But there are some promises that can't be kept' — he suddenly looked absurdly adult — 'if circumstances alter.' After that all that had to be decided was a plan of action. Katie agreed to stay on another day so that she and the Brigadier could visit Mr. Grey before laying the case before the authorities. Punishment of some kind there would have to be. Lindy had done untold harm. She had caused an agonising death, wrecked one marriage and maimed another two. Including mine, thought Katie, including mine; those letters spelled the end of spontaneity between Rhodri and me. She was out in the hall collecting her coat when

Barney suddenly materialised at her side.

'There's something much worse,' he said. 'I can't possibly tell you.'

★   ★   ★

The headmaster was a living portrait of his surname. Hair, suit, shirt and even his tie were grey. Nor was it a silver-grey, just the drab of a rainy day. He listened in silence while Brigadier Tolworthy talked. It was, Katie considered, a masterly summary of the facts. John Grey's first question was for her.

'Why did you go to Arnsbrueck?' he asked, harshly.

'I thought that anything I could find out about the mother could lead to understanding of the daughter.'

'And did you find out anything?' His voice was sarcastic.

'Not much,' she said honestly. But enough, she might have added, when you took into consideration all the other factors which added up to a deeply disturbed teenager. Mr. Grey, when questioned, admitted that his daughter had gone abroad on an exchange scheme but refused to specify the location except to the Special Investigation Branch. The Brigadier went off to make his report and Katie returned to the house. She spent the afternoon with Margaret, gardening, cooking, drinking tea, cementing a friendship which was to remain and endure. After tea she wandered across the lawn, out through the private gate and into the forest. It was time, she reckoned, that she did some thinking and she could only do that alone. She thought back — as she had so often the last couple of days — to the meeting with Patrick at Arnsbrueck.

★ ★ ★

That one unguarded moment was something she would remember all her life. Then they both started speaking simultaneously.

'Katie — you're in England. Or even America.'

'Patrick, I thought you'd gone to Cyprus!' In unconscious agreement, they wandered down the street towards the Bierhaus.

'I'm staying with the Tolworthys for a couple of days. Oh, it *is* good to see you.'

'Likewise. And I'm doing a stint here before embarking.'

'I heard about your engagement . . . '

'It's off.' He grinned ruefully. 'I suppose you could say it was never really on. My father thought he was dying and, naturally wanting the line to continue, talked to me about easing his path to the grave, the old hypocrite.' His tone was affectionate. 'Grania and I — well, she's quite a girl. Then I saw one day a light in her eyes that had never glowed for me and realised that a longed-for assignment was hers for the taking . . . ' They sat on a bench at a wooden table and toasted each other in Dortmünder beer.

'I've got so much to tell you,' exclaimed Katie. She didn't stop to analyse her reaction to what he'd just said. 'Most of it not very good,' she added.

'I heard about Brigadier Tolworthy's sister,' Patrick said.

'The whole story? Not the mystery woman?' She told him and he laughed at her as she sat there, living the rôle. Her face clouded.

'The bad part was Bill Ridley. He was special. He probably would have won the British Grand Prix eventually.' She lifted her mug to a deserted Silverstone. Patrick drank with her.

'Now we've just solved the poison-pen business. You can't possibly have heard about that yet!'

'I haven't. Tell me.' So she told him, that and a lot more, filling in the gaps that made up the days that ran into the weeks since they had last met. He talked about Rossmara and his family and people they knew there. Later they had ham rolls and more beer. And suddenly it was ten minutes to four. Patrick walked back with her to the Alter Markt.

'When are you joining Rhodri?' he asked. Katie thought of the low white house with the magnolia tree in the back yard. How far away it seemed.

'Soon,' she answered. There wasn't time to say any more. The army car drew up, Henry in the back. Patrick saluted the Brigadier. He dropped a light kiss on the top of Katie's head. Then he was gone.

★　★　★

The camp at Niederdorf had literally been built in a forest which once extended right through to the Belgian frontier. The engineers had been skilful: they had left as many trees as possible — trees to line the streets, woods between rows of houses — and had planted shrubs in all the gardens. The Tolworthys' house was on the perimeter. There were glades and clearings for the half-mile or so adjacent to human habitation. Undergrowth had been cleared, the sun pierced through the tops of the swaying pines. Another few hundred yards — and one was back in primeval forest. Katie wandered along paths trodden by thousands of feet before her, thinking of hopes for the future and things which had to be accepted in the present. She must have been nearly a mile from base when she discovered she was being followed.

She had stopped where two paths forked, wondering if the left-hand one eventually led back to the camp, when she had the sudden and most uncomfortable sensation of being watched. At that moment a twig snapped somewhere behind her. She realised with a shock of panic that not only was she alone and vulnerable at the approach of premature dusk but that an intruder stood between her and the safety of the Tolworthy house. She risked a glance over her shoulder and saw a shadow merge with the trunk of a pine. There was no sound except the whispering of the wind in the branches. No good turning back in the hope that other people would arrive in time to rescue her. She could only go on. She decided on the right-hand fork. From recollection of numerous journeys to and from the golf course, she knew that there were certain scheduled openings into the forest from the main Niederdorf-Tolrath road. In Germany tree-worship is a cult and therefore there is easy access. Broad rides led away from the road straight into the heart of the forest. The road was somewhere away to her right. All she had to do was to carry on till she hit one of the rides, then make a dash for the road. Once there, she could easily thumb a lift back into the camp. Imperceptibly, she hoped, she increased her speed. That, she immediately found out, was a mistake. Without looking round — and now she dared not look round — she knew that her pursuer had also quickened his footsteps.

Barney Fordyn had come to a decision. There was something he could not keep to himself any longer. Whatever the consequences, Katie Rees-Williams had a right to know. Making sure that he had the incriminating photograph in the back pocket of his jeans, he jumped on his bike and sprinted down the long, straight road which led to the edge of the camp and Brigadiers' Row. Henry, now back from his office, and Margaret were unsurprised to see him. After all, Katie was due to leave early the following morning.

'She's gone for a stroll in the woods,' said Margaret helpfully. 'If you're lucky you might meet her coming back.'

Someone once wrote a tune about walking in the Black Forest. It was gay and pretty and set the feet a-dancing. This wasn't gay and pretty at all and the feet were lumps of lead. Katie tried desperately to figure out how far it would be to the road but, ominously, there was no sound of traffic to guide her. To make matters worse, the light was deteriorating rapidly. Soon it would be dark and she would be lost. Once or twice she thought she heard a call but too far away and not in the direction of where she knew the road must be. Then, horrifyingly, she heard a noise much closer to hand, a sound that had been reproduced in countless films of violence — the snap of a flick-knife. At last she tried to run, stumbling through the undergrowth. Too late. The footsteps, the heavy breathing, were just behind her. In front there was nothing but near-darkness. There was another shout. With courage born of desperation, she stopped and turned round.

Barney had always looked a bit of a desperado. Now that he had filled out as well as growing taller in the last few months, that impression was intensified. The fact that his hair was falling lankly over his face and his teeth were bared in defiance added up to the

definite picture of a potentially danger-
ous man. Rape was obviously out as
long as he was hanging around. The
German youth decided that discretion
was the better part. He slithered into
the nearest thicket and disappeared.

9

'You must have been mad,' said Barney severely. '*Gerichts-verhandlung zur Feststellung der Todessursache-gasse* is the name the locals have for that bit of the forest.' He sounded as if anyone in their right mind would know something like that.

'What's that supposed to mean?' enquired Katie.

'Inquest Alley — because of all the bodies found there in the past.' He paused. 'Just a useful phrase to bandy around,' he said airily.

Barney, the hero, felt ten feet high and was correspondingly patronising. He could even feel sorry for Mrs. Rees-Williams, sipping brandy in front of the fire, unaware that another blow would shortly be hitting her. He thought again of the excitement of the chase. For the first time he wondered if playing with a rock group would fulfil his true personality . . . The Brigadier came back into the room.

'I've told your father that you're on your way home,' he said briskly. Barney came down to earth with a thud.

'Can — can I just have a last word?' he began. Katie went with him to the front door. When it came to what he had to do, he was life-size again, an adolescent schoolboy untypically bereft of words. Reluctantly he took the photograph from his pocket. He handed it over without a word.

Henry Tolworthy drove her to the airport next morning. On the way there, he was unusually expansive.

'That night I spent in England when Eleanor was killed . . . There was something, as I said, I could never tell Margaret, but I will tell you. I know you don't like loose ends.' He smiled at her. 'Even I suspected that the tensions engineered by my attitude to Jane might have affected Margaret and driven her to quite uncharacteristic behaviour. So I went to see her twin sister and put it to her. Incidentally, I had to stay the night as she lives on the Romney Marshes and I'd never have found the way back in the dark.' He paused for a moment. 'I could never let Margaret know I had doubts about her mental stability. Her sister Emily — sworn to secrecy, of course — convinced me entirely. That's when I began to see sense about Jane and Hans. Not approval — but a more liberal attitude.' In the departure lounge, he unexpectedly pecked at her cheek.

'Come and see us any time.'

She arrived in Sevenoaks at lunchtime to heartwarming welcome from her mother and all the children and a cable in an exotic envelope. 'Need you,' it read. 'When can you come?' It was signed Rhodri.

★ ★ ★

Mary Delaney had laid on a celebration dinner.

'When I saw that envelope,' she had explained, 'I realised I mightn't have you here much longer.' Katie, knowing that — whatever the fall of the dice — the statement was likely to be true, bit appreciatively into roast lamb with rosemary and imported new potatoes.

'Mother, have you ever thought of going back to Rossmara?' she hazarded. Mary didn't answer for a moment. Her thoughts went irresistibly to the everlasting beauty of the lakes and mountains of Killarney. There might be rain but it was soft rain, and the changing pattern of cloud and sunshine was mirrored in the water and chased across the hillsides. Later this month the gorse would be flaming gold, and the blooms of acacia and arbutus would follow. The purple heather of October would blend with the misty skyline. She only had to close her eyes and it was all there.

'I've thought of it,' she admitted, 'ever since I left. I can picture the place at any hour of day or night. But I know that it's always a mistake to go back. Houses look smaller, people are different, they grow away from you over the years. Most of all, I wouldn't want to be there without your father.' She sipped the wine Katie had brought back from Germany. 'Besides,' she went on, 'I've got used to Kent. I've even got fond of it. And I really am involved with all my children. One advantage of this job is that I can see them all grow up. I meet them in the High Street or in their parents' houses. Once in a while . . . ' she smiled reminiscently, 'I realise I've given one or two of them a push in the right direction.'

Privately she was worried about her daughter. Katie had shown her the contents of the cable but had appeared neither happy nor excited. Wasn't she pleased to be needed? Why hadn't she said something about arranging a flight to Washington? On the surface she was the same as always — relaxed, ready to laugh or sympathise. And yet . . . At that moment Katie got up to clear away the plates.

'I know exactly what you're thinking,' she said. 'Believe me, I'll tell you everything as soon as I possibly can.'

Katie had spent the afternoon in the flat; unpacking, dusting, doing the laundry. And all the time, one thought had stayed in the forefront of her mind; what a world of difference those two little words 'need you' would have made had she never seen the photograph Barney had taken from his pocket and passed speechlessly into her hand less than twenty-four hours earlier.

* * *

This was something she couldn't look on as just another link in the chain of events which had begun light years away last summer. This was a milestone in her life. As she unpacked, she thought back to the time she had practised a small deception and, in secret, agonised over it. How naïve she had been. How blind to what was happening to their marriage. Could it be that the first feeling of freedom that day on the Rhein had in reality been subconscious revolt against the strain of living up to Rhodri's personal standards? She was his, therefore she was perfect. He had put Maggy on a pedestal too — at the beginning. It was odd that a man of his intelligence should have such a blind streak about the women in his life.

While she absent-mindedly flicked a duster round the sitting-room, Katie found herself hoping sincerely that Maggy and Murdo were making out. It seemed even more important now than it had before. Rhodri hadn't recognised the name of Maggy Montgomery. Why should he? She had, after all, been precious to him only as Megan Rees-Williams. But it showed that he had let her drop completely out of his life. Just as she, Katie, would be forgotten? *I think*, Maggy had said, *he needs a challenge*. She had hesitated over the last word. Maggy had been kind. What she meant was that he needed, and probably always would need, the challenge of the younger generation. He would need to know, at first hand, why they thought and acted as they did. A younger woman would also provide the stimulus which was essential to keep his brain in top working order. And yet — now she came to think of it — it wasn't women who mattered to him most, it was his work. It was in his job that his interest and his sense of adventure really lay.

After she had loaded her washing machine, she sat down at the kitchen table and looked once again at the photograph Barney had given her. It had obviously been taken on the campus of an American college. In the foreground was Lindy Grey, the Lindy who made the most of what opportunities she had. Here she might have been a model posing for the All-American girl. She was wearing a tracksuit material dress — a knee-length shift, unbuttoned at the neck, in buttercup yellow. Long matching socks and yellow-and-white sneakers completed the picture. The American healthy look, casual but cared-for, showed in shining blown-back hair and white teeth against clear, tanned skin. In the background was a white-pillared building with steps leading up to wide glass doors. The figure leaning against one of the pillars was in profile, apparently unaware that a photograph was being taken. He wasn't the only person on the steps but he was instantly recognizable. It was Rhodri.

⋆ ⋆ ⋆

So that was poor Barney's dread secret. Presumably Lindy had sent him the picture, chiefly to show him what he was missing. Also, partly, out of mischief? But Barney hadn't been amused. He saw it as a threat to what seemed to be a happy marriage — and he couldn't make up his mind whether the whole thing would blow over (and anyway, Rhodri might just have been invited to coffee in the dorm) or to warn her, Katie, that she might be living in a fool's paradise. Sitting there, she suddenly recollected the day she had finally — and wrongly — deduced that Claire Fordyn must be the author of the poison-pen letters; she had glanced out of the kitchen window about the time Rhodri usually came home and saw him standing on the pavement. He had looked interested and diverted. Lindy Grey, whose head barely reached his shoulder, was smiling up at him. Katie had thought nothing of it at the time. Lindy, after all, was only a schoolgirl. But even then she was seventeen, wasn't she?

Katie wondered how they had met up again. Almost certainly it was Lindy's doing: she would have known she could get in touch with Rhodri via the British Embassy. Had she so soon become disenchanted with the American boys she met every day? Or had there always been a powerful attraction which had drawn her to Rhodri? However, the fact remained that he had responded to her initiative. Katie tried to imagine how Claire Fordyn must have felt — the outrage and jealousy she experienced when her husband turned to a much younger woman. But she couldn't feel anything. That would mean pre-judging the issue. What Lindy wanted, Lindy got, Claire had once remarked. Did that include Rhodri? Katie couldn't help remembering that he had once complained of Megan's lack of imagination. What was he going to think of Lindy's flights of fancy?

Before she went down to dinner with her mother, Katie stood at the living-room window. The sun had set and clouds were blowing up from the south-west, dark grey over rose pink, shifting and changing, dissolving at the centre to reveal a pocket of purest aquamarine. It was like the hush at the heart of the storm. Katie stood till all had faded to pearl. Then she went down the inside staircase to the main part of the house. As she went, she considered one outstanding question. Why the cable? She could only suppose that Rhodri had got in deeper than he had intended. Did he need his wife by his side as a polite reminder to possible successors of how far he intended to go? The answer came sooner than she had expected. On Saturday morning after breakfast she happened to glance out of the window which overlooked the laurels and the path giving on to Vine Court Road. A taxi had just drawn up at the gate. A man got out and stood with his back to her, paying the fare. Then he turned and looked straight up at the windows of the flat. She couldn't have moved back even if she had wanted to. She stood stock still and watched him open the gate, shut it again and take the path to the steps leading up to the front door of the flat. What price her theories now? Rhodri had come to find her because she hadn't answered his cable. He had come all the way from America because he needed her.

*   *   *

Mary Delaney had also seen the taxi draw up. The children didn't come on Saturdays so she had been mildly curious as to the identity of the visitor. When she recognised Rhodri, her first feeling had been of relief. Maybe things were going to work out after all. Surely her daughter's husband would not have travelled all this way without an overwhelming motive. Her only wish was for Katie to be happy and settled and have a family of her own. She knew that there were difficult periods in most marriages and her own had merely been the exception that proved the rule. It was also true that many were strengthened by overcoming the seemingly insuperable obstacles. She had sensed that Katie had come to a decision the last time Rhodri had stayed in Sevenoaks — a decision to give her marriage another chance. Mary washed up her breakfast mug and plate and hoovered briskly round the morning-room which was now her own private sanctum. As she passed the mantel-piece, she couldn't help stopping and picking up the wedding photograph of her only child. Was it only the young who looked at the camera with such smiling confidence? Long hair swept up in an adult gesture made her look even more vulnerable. And Rhodri? Touch-ingly delighted, yes — but could a man look over-possessive on his wedding day? Maybe she was indulging her imagination . . . She packed up the hoover and went out to the down-to-earth, everyday kitchen to make herself a prosaic cup of coffee.

The words that Katie had had in mind — whether said over the telephone or written in a letter — suddenly couldn't be uttered. It's not working out, she had wanted to say, because I made a mistake in the first place. Your sense of values is different from mine. What will happen to our marriage will be a slow process of erosion. I don't think I could stand that.

10

Now that he was in the same room with her, she noticed subtle differences in Rhodri's appearance. The shoes were American — well, why not? — his hair was shorter, he used expressions which had never been in his vocabulary before.

'You didn't call me,' he said. 'You didn't even apply for a stand-by passage or you'd have had to inform me. So I came over to get you.' Whatever the subtle alterations, there could be no doubt of his sincerity. He didn't try to touch her and for that she was momentarily grateful.

'I think you need me for the wrong reasons,' she answered. She hadn't intended to say that at all but as soon as the words were out of her mouth, she knew they were true. She went over to the handbag she'd slung into an armchair the previous night, opened it, pulled out her wallet, extracted the photograph Barney had given her. Silently, she handed it over. If Rhodri were surprised, he didn't show it.

'Oh, that!' he said flatly. 'I admit I was attracted. She's young, she's bright, she's got ideas . . . '

'Such as writing poison-pen letters?' suggested Katie. She saw his eyes narrow to glints of steel and took an involuntary step backwards. But he didn't move.

'Just because you did nothing about it at the time, you've been squaring your conscience by making deductions which have no basis in fact.'

'You're wrong on both counts.' Katie strove to keep her voice on a conversational level. 'I did everything I could because I was in love with you . . . ' She stopped, appalled at the tense she had used. Rhodri, mood changing, took a step forward, then another step. Now he was smiling, the old carefree challenging smile, and his arms were round her shoulders.

'You *are* still my wife, you know,' he said softly.

★   ★   ★

Mary Delaney was unhappy. The cup of coffee hadn't helped at all. She, who drank only socially, could have done with a stiff whisky-and-water to dispel her growing unease. It wasn't anything to do with the silence. From here on the ground floor, she would only have heard voices if they had been raised in anger. They might be making love, talking happily, having a drink, anything ... And yet she couldn't rid herself of a feeling of menace. She suddenly remembered, for no discernible reason, the evening Rhodri had taken them to dine at a pub in the High Street. When they returned to Vine Court Road, while Rhodri was garaging the car, she had nipped up to the flat to return to Katie the purse she had dropped getting out of the back seat. She heard the phone ringing as she passed through the open front door, and Katie answered it, but by the time she'd called out Katie was already in the bathroom with the taps turned on. So she had left the purse on the table just inside the living-room and gone down through the house to her own quarters. The odd thing was, though, that she could have sworn she'd had a glimpse of Rhodri coming out of the morning room where her own tele- phone was situated. She didn't know why she thought that impression was important, but she wished she could think of a way of talking to Katie on her own just for a moment.

Katie reminded herself that imper- turbability was her only weapon. She slipped from Rhodri's embrace without moving more than an unobtrusive step backwards. But he noticed. His hands clenched.

'Do you want to marry Lindy?' asked Katie calmly.

'No. I want her out of my hair,' said Rhodri shortly.

'So you want me back as a convenient shield?'

'No!' The word came out like an explosion. 'At one time I thought so. When I came back last time, I played that silly telephone trick on you — to put you in the wrong.' Katie understood, but only because she understood how her husband's mind worked. He wouldn't force her physically — his pride would never allow that. Instead he applied mental pressure. He had never asked her for an explanation of the poison-pen letters she had received; he had flipped them aside when engaging in the large issue. But she had to be persuaded to admit that she had snooped on him and he had hoped to frighten her into it by reproducing the circumstances. And yet — now he sincerely wanted her back. Till the next time someone younger drew him away again?

'Oh Rhodri!' She found she could

smile again. 'What am I going to do about you?'

* * *

Rain was pouring down at Heathrow. It lashed against the tall windows of the departure complex. The Pan-Am baggage check-in was crowded, people queuing back to the double doors of the entrance. Probably quite a few hoping for stand-by bargains, thought Katie, looking at the jeans and rucksacks. She was wearing her grey flannel suit with a white frilly-necked blouse and red high-heeled shoes. She turned away from the American line and handed her suitcase over to the Lufthansa desk.

Arnsbrueck was a small and newish airport. London's bad weather had given way to blue skies and fleecy clouds. Katie went through the turnstile into the arrival lounge and straight into Patrick's arms. Droning over the English channel, she remembered the day she had opened the door expecting to see Patrick — and Rhodri was there. That was when she knew, without any doubt, what her heart should have told her long, long ago. She and Patrick belonged together. She slid her arms round his neck as naturally as if they had been there many times before. His mouth came down to meet hers and her heart — it was true, it could happen — turned over. With Patrick there was no need to analyse, to explain. They loved and that was that. In his eyes, adultery was a sin and the little meannesses of the spirit forgiven. Patrick took her hand in his and led her out to the patio overlooking the airfield. Sunshine sparkled through the bottle of wine on the table with its gay striped umbrella. Goldener Oktober — what a lovely name for a wine. The slow, gentle ripening on the terraced hillsides, the harvesting of the grapes in the mellow light. Heady and yet serene. That's the way it would be with Patrick.

'Will you grow your hair again?' he said later. 'I don't want a mystery woman. I want the one I've always known.' Days later, he asked, 'Whatever happened to Lindy?'

'Lindy?' Katie came back to earth. 'Well, she was under age at the time. Also, she had committed no criminal offence. So it was decided to put her in custody of her father for a year. That should be punishment enough. But she's attending a German university at the same time, so there's a future for her if she'll take it.' Not much of an outlook for Veronica and John. None at all for Joanna. But the Fordyns and the Tolworthys survived. And Rhodri would find someone else. He probably had already.

'Rossmara for us?' said Katie dreamily. Well, that was the end of the rainbow. In the meantime, there was the whole world.

'Children,' said Patrick, 'are adaptable. Think of all the languages they'll pick up.' He smiled at her. 'As if it isn't the same in any language.'

We do hope that you have enjoyed reading this large print book.

Did you know that all of our titles are available for purchase?

We publish a wide range of high quality large print books including:
Romances, Mysteries, Classics
General Fiction
Non Fiction and Westerns

Special interest titles available in large print are:
The Little Oxford Dictionary
Music Book, Song Book
Hymn Book, Service Book

Also available from us courtesy of Oxford University Press:
Young Readers' Dictionary
(large print edition)
Young Readers' Thesaurus
(large print edition)

For further information or a free brochure, please contact us at:
Ulverscroft Large Print Books Ltd.,
The Green, Bradgate Road, Anstey,
Leicester, LE7 7FU, England.
Tel: (00 44) **0116 236 4325**
Fax: (00 44) **0116 234 0205**

Other titles in the
Linford Romance Library:

LOVE WILL FIND A WAY

Susan Darke

Sara is an hotel receptionist until her friend Caroline, a resident, helps her into a new job — as a secretary at her son Redvers' flower-farming business in the Scillies. When Redvers eventually whispered, 'I love you, Sara', she should have been elated. But an inner voice mocked her — telling her it would be more truthful had he said, 'I love you, *Miranda*' . . . Was he merely using her as a shield against a love that had once betrayed him?

FAR LIES THE SHORE

Marian Hipwell

Calanara was an island with a secret. What caused the rift between Tansy's mother and her grandfather? And why was the hostile Mark Harmon opposed to her plans for Whitton Lodge Nurseries? Probing past events helped Tansy to find solutions to the problems of the present, only to discover that there was no place for her on the island. Yet something about Calanara called to her and the longer she stayed, the harder it became to leave . . .

LOVE'S FUGITIVE

Rachel Ford

Exploring the French Pyrenees was meant to be a complete break for Victoria, as well as inspiration for possible future work, after her recent traumatic experiences . . . It didn't work out that way — drugged and robbed, she awoke to find herself at the mercy of Gilles Laroque! As lord of the manor he wielded considerable power: Victoria found herself trapped and made to 'pay her dues'. To an independent woman, the situation was unbearable . . .

DE OVING

Jean M. Long

Returning from holiday, Katie Mead discovers her business partner, Jack, has apparently vanished into thin air and a mysterious stranger, Lyall Travis, is lodging with her Aunt Alice . . . Despite reservations, Katie accepts Lyall's offer of help with her forthcoming jewellery exhibition. Theirs is a stormy relationship, for she suspects he was involved in Jack's disappearance. Katie enjoys Lyall's company, but her emotions must be kept in check until she has discovered the truth.